KATIE FRIEDMAN GIVES UP TEXTING!

Also by **Tommy Greenwald**

Charlie Joe Jackson's Guide to Not Reading
Charlie Joe Jackson's Guide to Extra Credit
Charlie Joe Jackson's Guide to Summer Vacation
Charlie Joe Jackson's Guide to Making Money
Jack Strong Takes a Stand

Tommy Greenwald

KATIE FRIEDMAN GIVES UP TEXTING!

And lives to tell about it.

Illustrations by J.P. Coovert

Roaring Brook Press ♥ New York

Text copyright © 2015 by Tommy Greenwald
Illustrations copyright © 2015 by J.P. Coovert
Published by Roaring Brook Press
Roaring Brook Press is a division of
Holtzbrinck Publishing Holdings Limited Partnership
175 Fifth Avenue, New York, New York 10010
mackids.com

Library of Congress Cataloging-in-Publication Data

Greenwald, Tom.
   Katie Friedman gives up texting! (and lives to tell about it.) / Tommy
Greenwald ; illustrated by J. P. Coovert. — First edition.
      pages cm
   Summary: "Charlie Joe Jackson's best friend Katie Friedman is tough, but can she
convince her fellow middle schoolers to give up their phones for a week?"—Provided
by publisher.
   ISBN 978-1-59643-837-8 (hardback)—ISBN 978-1-59643-839-2 (ebook)
   [1. Text messages (Cell phone systems)—Fiction.   2. Cell phones—Fiction.
3. Middle schools—Fiction.   4. Schools—Fiction.   5. Singers—Fiction.   6. Rock
music—Fiction.   7. Humorous stories.]   I. Coovert, J. P., illustrator.   II. Title.
   PZ7.G8523Kat 2015
   [Fic]—dc23

                                                                    2014037585

Roaring Brook Press books may be purchased for business or promotional use. For
information on bulk purchases please contact Macmillan Corporate and Premium
Sales Department at (800) 221-7945 x5442 or by email at
specialmarkets@macmillan.com.

First edition 2015
Book design by Andrew Arnold
Printed in the United States of America by RR Donnelley & Sons Company,
Harrisonburg, Virginia
10 9 8 7 6 5 4 3 2 1

To the entire, extended Utz family
especially Mama Rose

INTRODUCTIONS

Hey, everyone—nice to see you. It's me, Katie Friedman.

You guys remember me, right?

I'm the one who's usually cheering on the sidelines while Charlie Joe Jackson tells you all those heroic stories about how awesome he is. But he's not all that awesome. He's lazy, conceited, and obnoxious. He's also been my best friend since kindergarten.

♥ ♥ ♥

But enough about him.

Let's talk about me.

♥ ♥ ♥

I have an important question to ask you.

Are you doing something else besides reading this book right now?

Are you texting, or Instagraming, or watching a TV show online, or anything like that?

Are you FaceTiming with anyone?

Are you checking Facebook? Snapchat? Twitter?

Are you on Face-Twit-Chat-Gram?

I know, Face-Twit-Chat-Gram doesn't exist.

Yet.

But it might by the time I finish writing this book.

Or you finish reading it.

Can I ask you something else?

Are you ever worried that screens might run your life? And maybe ruin your life, too?

I didn't think so.

I wasn't worried, either.

I should have been.

Part 1
JANE'S DEAL

A BUSY MORNING

Here's what happened *before* breakfast on Monday, April 23:

I texted Hannah Spivero: `I need to talk to you at lunch.`

She texted me back: `About what?`

I texted her back: `Stuff`

She texted me back: `What kind of stuff?`

I texted her back: `Nareem stuff.`

She texted me back. `Got it. KK`

I posted a picture of my dog staring at herself in the mirror.

I got a text from Becca Clausen: Mom says yes to rehearsal wednesday

I texted her back: Yay! Lots to do! Talent show in two weeks! Should we rehearse Saturday, too?

She texted me back: Dunno, might have basketball

I texted her back: Noooooooo

♥ ♥ ♥

Then I texted Charlie Joe Jackson: Ugh

He texted me back: What?

I texted him back: Nareem thing

He texted me back: Oooh

♥ ♥ ♥

Then I got in the shower.

♥ ♥ ♥

Here's what happened *during* breakfast on Monday, April 23:

I got a text from Nareem Ramdal: Hey

I texted him back: Hey

He texted me back: See you at school

I texted him back: Yup

6

♥ ♥ ♥

Then I got a text from Eliza Collins: `Hi Katie!`

I texted her back: `Hi`

She texted me back: `Did you do the math?`

I texted her back: `Yes`

She texted me back: `Can i take a quick look in homeroom?`

I texted her back: `Again?`

She texted me back: `Last time i swear!!!`

I texted her back: `I guess`

She texted me back: `You're the best!`

♥ ♥ ♥

I texted Hannah: `Eliza is driving me crazy`

Hannah texted me back: `Duh`

I texted Hannah back: `Can't take it anymore.`

♥ ♥ ♥

Then I texted Becca: `Can Sammie bring her drums to rehearsal?`

I got a text back: `Dunno will ask her`

Then I looked up and saw my parents looking at me.
They were both shaking their heads.

♥ ♥ ♥

Here's what happened *on the bus ride to school* on Monday,
April 23:

I texted Charlie Joe: `Eliza is so annoying`
`sometimes`

I got a text from Charlie Joe: `Sometimes?`

♥ ♥ ♥

Then I texted my mom: `Are you picking me up`
`after school?`

She texted me back: `Can't, working, take`
`bus okay?`

I texted her back: `K`

She texted me back: `K is not a word, and stop texting in school.`

I texted her back: `I'm on the bus`

She texted me back: `Got to go, love you honey.`

I texted her back: `K`

She texted me back: `Very funny.`

I got another text from Charlie Joe: `Good luck with the Nareem thing`

I texted him back: `THX gonna need it`

Then we got to school, and the day began.

THE NAREEM THING

"The Nareem thing," in case you're wondering, was me thinking I might break up with my boyfriend, Nareem Ramdal.

Nareem and I had been going out for nine months, which is approximately eight months and twenty-one days longer than the average middle school relationship. But that's not why I thought it was maybe time to break up.

I thought it was maybe time to break up because I wasn't sure I liked him anymore. You know—*liked him* liked him.

Hannah ended up asking me about it at lunch. "What was the Nareem stuff you wanted to talk about?" she whispered.

"I'm thinking of breaking up with him," I whispered back.

"Hey, no secrets you two," said Celia Barbarossa, who

was sitting next to Hannah. "Especially if it involves the opposite sex. Anything you need to tell us?"

"Maybe," I said. "It's about Nareem. He's awesome, of course. I just think that maybe, you know, it's time."

"Why would you want to break up with Nareem?" Hannah asked. "He's like the greatest guy on earth."

I was pretty sure that Hannah didn't think that Nareem was the greatest guy on earth. I was pretty sure that Hannah thought *Jake Katz* was the greatest guy on earth. Hannah and Jake were the current world record-holders for longest middle school couple—they'd been going out for almost two years. Everybody was pretty sure they were going to get married.

"Well, the thing is—" I said, but then I stopped.

Hannah was texting.

I looked around at the rest of the table—Jake, Phil Manning, Celia Barbarossa, Timmy McGibney, and Jessica Greenfield.

Everyone was staring at their phones. They were either texting, Instagraming, playing a game, or loading some app that had just been invented.

Jessica texted something and laughed; then Celia read something and laughed.

So, those two weren't just texting. They were texting each other.

I'm sure I had a very irritated look on my face, but it didn't matter, since no one was looking at me. "Seriously, you guys?"

No response. I said again, "Seriously?"

One or two heads looked up.

"What?" said Jessica.

"What do you mean, 'what'?" I said. "I'm trying to talk about something important."

"We're totally listening," said Phil, who totally wasn't.

"Forget it," I said.

Hannah felt bad, I could tell, but not that bad—a little bad. "No, come on Katie, I really am listening. Tell us about Nareem." I could feel her pushing SEND while she said it.

"Yep, I agree, Katie, Nareem is totally awesome," added Celia, who never took her eyes off her phone.

I could feel my ears start to burn with frustration.

"THAT'S NOT EVEN WHAT I SAID!" I said, loudly.

That got everybody's attention.

"You guys are so annoying," I added, not as loudly.

"What do you mean, we're annoying?" asked Timmy. "Everybody uses their phone at lunch. That's what we do. You use yours just as much as anyone else."

"This stuff is important," Phil pointed out. "My followers count on me." He showed Timmy a picture, and they both cracked up.

"Whatever," I said. "I don't usually just sit there like a robot and text people sitting right next to me!"

"Yes, you do," Jake said, unhelpfully.

I thought about arguing some more, but I didn't. He was right. I usually texted all during lunch, too. Everybody texted at lunch, because it was the only time you were allowed to use your phone at school. But this was different. I had something important to discuss, and I wanted to actually *talk* about it.

"Okay fine, maybe I text at lunch sometimes, but now that I see you guys doing it, it looks really stupid."

"You're right, it's stupid," said Hannah, actually putting away her phone. That made everybody else put away their phones, too. Hannah was kind of a leader that way. "We're sorry."

"Let's talk about Nareem," added Timmy.

"I don't want to talk about it anymore," I said. Yes, I admit it—I was being childish.

Someone came up behind me—I turned around to see my friend Becca Clausen, who always seemed to be there when I needed her most.

I looked up at her—which was a long way up, by the way, because she was like seven feet tall.

"What's wrong?" she said.

13

"How could you tell something was wrong?"

"I know you," she said. "That, and the fact that your face is twitching."

Apparently my face twitches when I get upset.

I got up and walked toward the drink machines. Becca followed.

"I think I might break up with Nareem," I told her. "But I feel really badly about it."

"Why?"

"Why what? Why am I breaking up with him? Or why do I feel badly about it?"

"Both, I guess."

I thought for a second. "I'm breaking up with him because I don't really like him that way anymore. And I feel bad because I still like him another way."

"As a friend."

"Yeah."

Becca nodded. "That makes complete sense."

See? Some friends just get you.

Ms. Ferrell, my guidance counselor, came over to get a drink. "I'm counting on you guys for the talent show," she told us. "It's a week from Saturday!"

Becca and I started a band last year, called CHICK-MATE. Being in a band was kind of the most awesome thing that had ever happened to me.

"Yup," Becca said. "We're rehearsing Wednesday."

Ms. Ferrell smiled. "Terrific! I'm really looking forward to seeing you play. First stop, the talent show. Next stop, world tour!"

"Ha-ha," I said.

"Ha-ha yourself," said Ms. Ferrell, winking as she walked away.

Becca and I looked at each other.

"What was that about?" I asked.

Becca shook her head. "I have no idea. Maybe she heard we were good or something."

"From who?"

Becca's phone buzzed, and she took it out. She read a text and started giggling.

"What?" I asked.

"Nothing," said Becca. "Just Jackie." Jackie was our keyboard player. Becca asked her to join the band because they played basketball together. Jackie wasn't the greatest musician in the world, but she was really funny—and besides, in middle school you take what you can get.

I watched Becca text for a minute, then got bored. "I'm going back to the table."

"Okay," Becca said, giggling at another text from Jackie or somebody.

I went back over and sat down. Everybody put away their phones as soon as they saw me coming.

"Do you still want to talk about the Nareem thing?" asked Hannah. "My phone is totally in my pocket, in case you do."

"So is mine," said Phil. "Way down in my pocket. I'm completely available to talk about some deep, heavy stuff."

He laughed, as did Timmy and Jake. Boys are so annoying, when they're not awesome.

"No, I'm fine," I said. "Thanks, though."

Which was right when Nareem walked up.

"Hey," he said.

"Hey," I said back.

"What are you guys talking about?"

"Nothing."

"Really?"

I nodded. Then I took out my phone and started texting, just like everybody else.

CHANGE OF PLANS

After spending all math period thinking about what to do, I decided to definitely, absolutely, positively break up with Nareem.

In a text.

Not exactly brave, I know. But I wanted to get it over with, so the next period, when we were both in study hall, I texted him—which was completely illegal, by the way.

Me: `There's something i need to tell you.`

Him: `Okay, i have something to tell you, too.`

Wow. All of a sudden I felt a little nauseous. Was he going to break up with me first?

I put away my phone and walked quickly over to his table. When he saw me coming, he smiled, and I immediately knew he wasn't breaking up with me at all.

"I have amazing news," he said.

"What?"

He sat up straight, to demonstrate the importance of what he was about to say. "Do you want to go see Plain Jane with me tomorrow night?"

Wait a second.

Did he just say *Plain Jane*??

Whoa!!

I'm not proud to admit it, but that changed everything.

You have to understand: Plain Jane is my favorite band. They're just like CHICKMATE. They're all girls; they seem like they're all good friends; and they have a great time.

And get this: their lead singer, Jane Plantero, grew up in Eastport, and even went to our middle school!

So basically, the only way we're different is that they're rock stars and we're not.

"Plain Jane?" I said, probably too loudly for study hall. "You got tickets to Plain Jane? On a school night?"

Nareem looked down shyly, the way he always did when he felt proud about something. "Yes. Also, if you would like, we have been invited to go backstage and meet the band after the concert."

OMG, I thought, *I can't believe I was ever considering breaking up with you.*

I hugged him. "Are you kidding?!"

"Quiet, you two," said Mrs. Argentino, the study hall monitor.

"Backstage passes?" I whispered. "Seriously, truly, and honestly?"

"Yes," Nareem whispered back, his eyes wide. He didn't want to get Mrs. Argentino mad. He didn't want to get anyone mad.

"Because of your dad?"

"Yes. Shhh."

Nareem's father is a lawyer who works in the music business. That's all I knew, until that second. If I knew he could get us backstage passes to Plain Jane concerts, I would have asked him a lot more questions about his career, and probably washed his car and taken out his garbage a few times.

I put my hand on Nareem's arm. "I would love to go," I said. "You are so incredibly sweet to invite me. Thank you so much."

"You're welcome," Nareem said, blushing slightly. "And now, we should probably get to work before Mrs. Argentino becomes angry."

As I watched Nareem open his backpack and take out his homework, I thought about the concert, and I got more and more excited. I felt so happy. I felt so grateful that Nareem would do this for me. I felt so lucky to be going out with him.

It's interesting, the tricks your mind can play on you when it wants to.

A CONVERSATION, KIND OF

I bumped into Charlie Joe in the hallway on the way to my next class.

"How was study hall?" he asked.

"Fine."

"Was Nareem there?"

"Yup."

"What did you guys talk about?"

"Not much."

We stared at each other awkwardly.

It would have been easier to just text Charlie Joe, so we could have a real conversation. If we'd been texting, he could have said ARE YOU EVER GOING TO BREAK UP WITH NAREEM OR NOT? And I could have answered, I WILL WHEN THE TIME IS RIGHT! STOP ASKING ME! YOU'RE BEING ANNOYING!

But we weren't texting each other, so we couldn't say any of those things.

Charlie Joe started to walk away. "So, uh, I'll talk to you later," he said.

"He invited me to a concert," I blurted out.

Charlie Joe stopped. "What concert?"

"Plain Jane."

"Wow, you totally love them."

"I know, I do."

We looked at each other. I think he could read my mind. That I wouldn't be breaking up with Nareem after all. And not necessarily for the right reasons.

But all he said was, "Text me later."

And all I said was, "Okay."

5

DON'T CONTROL, CONNECT!

The first thing you notice at a concert is the noise. It's like an airplane taking off, over and over again. You hear it before you even walk into the arena.

The second thing you notice is the arena itself. Huge. Filled with thousands of people. Mostly girls like me, between the ages of ten and twenty I think. Which is the age when our lungs are working at maximum capacity.

I guess what I'm saying is, the place was *loud*.

Before we went inside, Mr. Ramdal pulled me, Nareem, and Nareem's little sister Ru aside.

"WE STICK TOGETHER!" he yelled over the crowd. "NO ONE LEAVES MY SIGHT!" At least that's what I think he said. He might have said, "NO ONE LEAVES MY *SIDE*!" Same difference.

"OKAY!" we all yelled back.

Then Mr. Ramdal gave us these bracelets to put on,

which immediately turned us into incredibly important people. It got us through about eight security checks and down about three levels of stairs until we ended up seven rows from the stage.

I turned around and saw about 14,000 people with worse seats than me. It's easy to feel pretty superior when that happens.

We got to our seats just before eight, which was five minutes before the show was supposed to start. Then we waited for an hour.

"THIS HAPPENS SOMETIMES," Nareem's father shouted, as warm-up music blasted away. "MUSIC PEOPLE ARE LATE QUITE OFTEN. FOR MEET-INGS AS WELL AS FOR CONCERTS."

We nodded, staring at everything, including our bracelets.

At exactly nine o'clock, the lights went out.

Then it sounded like a thousand planes taking off at the same time.

Planes with huge engines, and filled with thousands of screaming teenage girls.

I heard someone plunk some notes on a guitar, then someone bang a drum a few times. My heart started to race.

Then, all of a sudden . . . BAM!

The music exploded.

The first chords of "Life Is for the Living" began, one of my favorite Plain Jane songs. Lights flashed everywhere, then suddenly, the band was right in front of us—no more than thirty feet away! My eyes zeroed in on Jane Plantero, guitarist and lead singer. She sang right to me. I swear.

Don't control—connect.
Don't attack—accept.
Gifts are for the giving.
Life is for the living.

The whole audience was singing along, of course. I was probably singing louder than anyone—except when I was posting pictures online. I think everyone was doing some sort of online bragging. It's definitely the best way of saying to your friends, *I'm here and you're not.*

The song ended, and the crowd went wild.

Jane stepped up to the microphone.

"Hey, what's up Connecticut? So glad to be back in the old neighborhood!"

The crowd answered with a sound louder then planes taking off. It was more like the sound of a rocket launching.

Then Jane put her hands out and motioned for quiet.

"I have a favor to ask you guys."

The crowd actually got quieter. Not quiet, but quieter.

"I want to ask you guys to help me make music tonight."

The crowd got *un*-quiet quickly, until Jane put her hands out again.

"I want you guys to help me make some beautiful music by taking it a little easy with those phones, and those cameras, those doo-hickeys and devices and gizmos and gadgets. Let's just sing together. Let's connect. Let's make eye contact. Let's make history. Let's make music."

I suddenly realized I had my phone out, recording her speech about putting away our phones. When I looked around, I saw that 14,000 other people were doing the same thing.

"Sound cool?" Jane asked.

Everyone roared.

"SHE WANTS US TO CONNECT!" I screamed to Nareem.

"I KNOW!" Nareem yelled back.

His father just shook his head and smiled.

I put away my phone. Nareem put away his phone. Ru was too young to have a phone.

I was able to listen to one whole song before I took out my phone and started texting and taking video again.

6

BACKSTAGE

After the concert, which was *unbelievably unbelievable,* our magic bracelets became even more magical.

First, a very large man came over and whispered something to Nareem's dad. Then he nodded at us, and we all followed him past the stage, down a long dark corridor and up to a big gold door that said ARTIST on it.

The very large man knocked.

The door opened.

Another very large man stuck his head out. Nareem's father showed him his bracelet. The second very large man nodded.

And just like that, we were in.

Backstage!!!!

Food everywhere. Candy everywhere. Soda everywhere. Beer everywhere. People everywhere. *Famous* people everywhere. All wearing the very same bracelets we had on.

The four of us stood there for a minute with our mouths on the ground until a very young, very pretty woman wearing the nicest jacket I've ever seen—it was red and gold, with the Plain Jane logo stitched across the back—came up to us.

She gave Nareem's father a hug, and he immediately became the coolest parent I knew. By a long shot.

"Mr. Ramdal, so good to see you."

Nareem's dad nodded shyly. He wasn't really the hugging type, as far as I could tell. "You as well, Kit."

Kit smiled at the rest of us. "Hi, guys, I'm Kit St. Claire. Come on back and meet the band."

We gave each other a look like "Are you kidding me?!" and then followed Kit down another, shorter hallway. There was another door, except this one was bright red, and the sign on it said PLAIN JANE. Kit didn't knock, she just opened the door.

The first thing I saw was Jane Plantero, half undressed. OMG!

We were all about to turn away, but she looked up and smiled.

"Hey, my man Sanjay!"

It took me a minute to realize that Nareem's father's first name must be Sanjay.

"Are these your kids?" asked Jane, as she put the rest of her non-concert clothes on.

"These two, Nareem and Ru," Mr. Ramdal said. Then

he pointed at me. "This is Nareem's friend and your biggest fan."

Jane shook all our hands. "You guys are all from Eastport, huh? My old stomping grounds?"

We all nodded.

"Your dad is a genius," Jane said to Nareem and his sister. "He's probably kept me out of jail more than once or twice."

"She's kidding," Mr. Ramdal said quickly.

Jane looked at me. "What's your name, sweetie?"

"Katie," I said, or at least tried to.

"Well, hey, Katie. Thanks for buying the merch."

"Merch?" I asked, confused.

Jane pointed at my Plain Jane sweatshirt. "Merchandise, baby. That's what pays the bills these days, ever since the record business blew up." She looked at Mr. Ramdal. "Sanjay taught me that."

I couldn't believe Nareem's father, who'd always been this quiet, polite man, picking his son up after student government, was good friends with my favorite rock star. Boy, life can sure surprise you sometimes.

"Katie is in a band," Nareem said, out of nowhere.

Jane's eyebrows went up. "Is that right?"

"They're really good," Nareem added, realizing that I was too embarrassed to talk about it. "They play a bunch of your songs."

"I know every song you've ever written by heart," I blurted out, for some reason.

"Sweet!" Jane said. "Do you write your own songs, too?"

That was a tricky question. I'd started fooling around with lyrics a bit, but didn't have the guts to show them to anyone.

"Not yet," I answered. "I want to, though."

Jane stared at me, her intense eyes burning. "Don't 'want!' Do!"

"If I can write one song in my lifetime half as beautiful as 'Your Heartbreak or Mine,'" I told her, "I will be the happiest person who ever lived."

"Aw, now you're just being nice," Jane said.

I shook my head. "No, I'm not. I really think it's just the most perfect song ever written."

"Well, look at you, sneaky little thing!" Jane said, laughing. "Flattery will get you everywhere!"

"We should go," Mr. Ramdal said. "You have many people who want to visit with you, I'm sure." I stared at him, crushed—betrayed by this man who had been my hero for the last three hours.

"In a minute," Jane said. "So, let me ask you guys something. That stuff I said about taking it easy with the phones and the gadgets. How'd it sound? Did I come off okay, or did I sound like a school principal?"

Was Jane actually asking for *our* advice?

"I thought it was great," Nareem said. "You were completely correct."

"Yeah," I agreed. "People were spending so much time on the phones they practically missed the whole concert!"

Jane's eyes twinkled. "Not you guys, though, right?"

We all stared at our shoes and said some variation of "Um."

Then she winked and let out a huge laugh. "Ah, I'm just giving you a hard time!"

Kit came up and whispered something in Jane's ear. "Well, duty calls," Jane said to us. "Got some other folks that need tending to."

I looked around, wondering who the other folks were, since there was no one else inside that private room. Not even the rest of the band.

Kit started steering Jane out the door, but as she passed me, she stopped and grabbed my arm. "Hey, you! Flattery girl! You write a song, and you send it to me," Jane called back to me. "I wanna hear what you got." She winked at Mr. Ramdal. "The money man knows how to find me."

Then just like that she was out the door, plunged into the crazy world of post-concert rock-star life.

Wow.

"That was so cool," Nareem said. "She really seemed to like you."

"Hey, Nareem?" I said.

He looked up from his drink. "Yes?"

"Just . . . thanks."

"For what?"

I couldn't decide whether to say "For taking me to the concert," or "For telling Jane I was in a band," or "For not minding that she talked more to me than to you," so instead I just said, "For everything."

Nareem smiled. "You're welcome."

Ru had one more question for her dad. "Are we going to meet the rest of the band?"

Some people are never satisfied.

Meanwhile, I tried to understand what had just happened. Jane was amazing. She was exciting. She was inspiring. She was scary. And she may have been the most important thing that had ever happened to me.

As we headed out of the arena, I knew one thing for sure.

I was going to write that song.

TWO LIES IN TWO MINUTES

On the car ride home, we listened to Plain Jane songs until finally Mr. Ramdal told us he couldn't take it anymore and turned on the news.

Nareem took that opportunity to ask me the question I'd been waiting for.

"What did you want to talk to me about?"

My first plan was to play dumb. "Huh?"

"In study hall yesterday," Nareem reminded me (as if I needed reminding). "You said you wanted to talk to me about something, but then I told you about the Plain Jane concert, and you never told me."

"Oh, right." I moved on to my second plan. "I just wanted to tell you that I was sorry I was kind of rude to you at lunch. Everyone was texting instead of talking, and I started to get annoyed."

First lie.

"People text instead of talk all the time," Nareem pointed out.

"I know, but I think it's starting to get out of control."

"You sound like Jane," Nareem said, smiling. "Don't control—connect!"

"Well, she's right, don't you think?"

Nareem shrugged. "Sure, if you say so."

Right at that moment, of course, I got a text. I ignored it, which wasn't easy. Anybody knows that ignoring an unread text, when it's just sitting there on your phone, is one of the hardest things to do in the entire world.

"You got a text," Ru announced, unnecessarily.

"You're not going to read it?" Nareem asked.

"No."

He started to laugh. "Come on. Get it. You know you want to."

"I don't! Seriously, I don't."

We rode in silence for a minute until finally I said, "Fine," and pulled out my phone.

It was from Charlie Joe.

`How was the concert with your not-ex-boyfriend?`

I put my phone away.

"Who was it?" Nareem asked.

I shook my head. "My mom, just wanting to know when I'd be home."

Second lie.

I'd never lied to Nareem before, and now I had told him two lies in two minutes.

Not a good sign.

MEET THE PARENTS

The first thing I did when I got home was obsess over the pictures and videos I took at the concert.

Then I posted them online and sat back, waiting for all the comments and likes to start pouring in.

Which is when my mom poked her head in.

"Are you going to tell us about the concert?"

"In a minute."

She sighed as she walked away.

Listening to her sigh, I sighed.

I should probably mention that my mom and dad are both therapists. They're big into communication and connection. Kind of like Plain Jane, but without the power chords.

Which is great, usually, and I love them and we get along really well, but sometimes they're a little bit more into communication than I want them to be, and sometimes they ask too many questions.

And sometimes, a single question is too many.

A few minutes later, my mom knocked again.

"Hold on," I called.

The third time, a couple of minutes after that, my dad was with her. This time they wouldn't take no for an answer.

"Tell us about how tonight went," they said, marching into my room.

"It was awesome," I answered, not taking my eyes off my computer. Responses were starting to come in to my concert report—mostly saying various versions of *"OMG I am so jealous!!!"*—and I wanted to be able to read every one of them.

My dad walked up and peered over my shoulder at my computer screen.

"Are you on Facebook?"

"Yes, Dad."

"I thought we agreed no Facebook until high school."

"We did, but then I told you that tons of other kids have it, and if I didn't get it I would become socially isolated." Sometimes you have to talk to a therapist in their own language—especially if it's your dad.

"How much time a day do you spend on this thing?"

"Almost none," I said, which wasn't technically totally true.

"Between the phone and the computer," said my mom, "we barely see you anymore."

"And you're not even in high school yet," my dad added, piling on.

"Listen, this is how kids communicate these days," I said. "It's crazy to fight it. You would have actually been proud of me at lunch yesterday, I got mad at the other kids because they were texting when I was trying to tell them something. But everybody basically laughed at me."

Right on cue, I got a text, which I glanced at quickly. It was from Charlie Joe: 46 LIKES ALREADY!

"Oooh, nice going," said my mom.

I rolled my eyes. "People just think it's cool that I went to the concert and met Jane."

"Well, don't be too braggy," she said. "People don't like braggarts."

I KNOW! I typed back to Charlie Joe, with my two thumbs. I was the fastest two-thumb typer in the country, by the way. I don't know that for a fact, but it's hard to believe anyone was faster than me.

Charlie Joe and I exchanged about five more texts in the next minute. My parents watched me the whole time, shaking their heads.

"Unbelievable," my dad said. "Does it ever stop?"

"I think unlimited texting was a mistake," my mom said.

"I need to check your computer," my dad said.

"What?!" I put my phone away and shut my laptop. "Don't you guys trust me? I get good grades, I'm normal, I'm nice, I empty the dishwasher—what else do you want from me?"

My mom sat down on the bed next to me and kissed my cheek.

"A short description of the concert would be nice," she said.

DIFFERENT DREAMS

There were four of us in CHICKMATE: myself on guitar and lead vocals; Becca Clausen, who started the band with me, on guitar and background vocals; Jackie Bender on keyboards; and Sammie Corcoran on drums. We were still looking for a bass player. Turns out there aren't a lot of bass players in middle school—especially girl bass players.

Wednesday night, the night after the Plain Jane concert, we had rehearsal. We usually rehearsed in Becca's basement, because it was soundproof—which was very important to parents—and because it was big enough to hold instruments, amps, drums, and five-foot-ten-inch Becca Clausen.

I got there early, and Becca waved me into the kitchen, where she was eating cereal. "Want some?"

I shook my head. "No thanks, I'm good."

I watched her eat for another minute.

"Okay, I guess I'll have a little."

Becca laughed. "No one can resist the power of Froot Loops." She was right about that.

I helped myself and started chomping away. After a minute Becca said, "I still can't believe you met Plain Jane."

"I didn't actually meet the whole band," I said between bites. "Just Jane."

Becca laughed. "Katie, she *is* the band. She's the lead singer and she writes the songs. It's all her."

"I guess." After a few more bites, I decided to bring up the topic of conversation that I'd been thinking about all day, and the reason I decided to get there early. "So, speaking of writing songs, I was . . . I think we should write one for the talent show."

Becca stopped eating and looked at me. "Write a song? Us?"

"Yeah."

She laughed. "I don't know. I'm not a songwriter. I'm not even a real musician, the way you are. I'm a basketball player who plays a little bit of guitar."

"That's not true."

"Besides, at talent shows people want to hear songs they know," Becca said. "What if we write something terrible and everyone laughs at us?"

I was afraid of that, too, but I remembered what Jane said about taking chances and tried to put any doubts out of my head. "That won't happen," I said.

She put the milk away just as the doorbell rang. "Let's ask Jackie and Sammie."

I felt myself getting frustrated. "I don't care about Jackie and Sammie, Becca. I want to know what *you* think. You and I started this band, and we can decide what we want to play. Doing an original song would be so fun and cool. I know it's risky. But let's do it." I saved the best for last. "And guess what? If it's good, Jane said she would listen to it!"

Becca laughed. "Oh, right," she said. "Jane Plantero is going to listen to some song written by a couple of kids. Why would she do that? Just because she went to the same school as us?"

"Because she said she would," I insisted.

"Whatever," Becca said. "Let's just go rehearse."

The front door opened, and Jackie and Sammie came into the room. "Froot Loops!" Sammie yelled excitedly.

"Help yourself," said Becca, getting the milk out again. But her smile was a little forced, and I could tell she was kind of mad at me.

As the other girls chomped away, I pulled Becca aside. "I saw Jane up there, and as I watched her, singing her own songs, it was like I was watching a dream," I whispered. "And it made me realize dreams come true. We can do this. I know we can."

Becca started putting the bowls in the dishwasher. "Well, maybe that's the thing."

"What's the thing?"

She stopped and looked at me.

"Your dream might not be my dream," she said.

We rehearsed for an hour and a half, and neither of us said another word about writing songs.

THE LAST TEXT

"Katie? Everything okay in there?"

I was at home in the bathroom, and I had the shower running.

"What? I can't hear you!"

"You've been in the shower a long time!"

"Okay, I'm getting out!"

The truth was, I hadn't been in the shower at all. I'd been texting my friends. It was an hour after rehearsal, and there was a lot to discuss. But if I'd been in my room, my parents would have done what they did the other night, knocking every five seconds and looking over my shoulder.

So I decided to "take" a shower. And my mom wanted to know why it was taking so long to get clean.

"You're wasting water!"

"In a minute!"

My phone beeped—incoming. I was mainly texting three people: Becca, Nareem, and Charlie Joe. I was talking to Becca about the talent show, avoiding the topic of writing songs; I was complaining to Nareem that Becca didn't want to write songs; and I was telling Charlie Joe that Nareem was a great boyfriend because he listened without judging.

Are you saying I judge? asked Charlie Joe.

Stop jumping to conclusions, I answered. Nareem is just nicer than you, that's all.

He wrote back immediately: Hey!

"Katie!" It was my dad. "Turn that thing off!"

You can't pressure her. From Nareem.

I'm not! I just thought writing songs would be cool.

Becca: Sorry about today. Don't be mad.

So, she wanted to talk about the songwriting thing after all.

I immediately wrote her back. i'm totally not mad!

Phew, she wrote back. I don't want to hold you back. If you want to start another band with more serious musicians i would totally understand.

Cut it out, I wrote. i'm a CHICKMATER
for life.

HA-HA, Becca wrote.

Another knock on the door. I turned the shower off.
"I'm drying my hair!"

"For crying out loud," muttered my dad.

I needed to wrap this up.

TTYL XX, I texted Becca.

Becca and I just made up! I texted
Nareem.

A text from Charlie Joe: Well i'm glad you
still like Nareem. It actually makes
life a lot less complicated. I mean
it.

A text from Nareem. Yay!

"What exactly are you doing in there?" my mom asked.

"I think we need to talk about possibly limiting your
phone time," said my dad. "Enough is enough. This is
absurd."

"Coming!" I yelled.
"I swear!"

"Now!" my dad yelled back.

"I can't believe this!" I screamed. "I'm not doing anything wrong!"

"Hurry up!"

I stared down at the phone, my heart pounding. My parents were really getting on my nerves, but if I didn't get out of there, I was going to lose my phone privileges. I quickly typed out one last text.

`I didn't say I still liked Nareem. I said he was a great boyfriend. LOL! G2G`

I hit send.

Then I unlocked the bathroom door, walked by my parents with a smile, went into my room, and lay down on my bed.

My parents stood at the doorway and watched me.

"We just think it's getting too much," my mom said, quietly.

I stared at the ceiling. "What's getting too much?"

"You know," said my dad.

"You guys don't understand," I said. "It's how kids communicate today. It is. Everyone does it. I told you that."

My mom took a deep breath. "We do understand," she said. "That's what we're afraid of. It's kind of communicating, but it's also not. It's also hiding behind something. It's not completely real."

I rolled my eyes. "Whatever. It's real to me."

My phone beeped.

Incoming text.

I didn't move.

"Aren't you going to get it?" asked my dad.

"No."

It beeped again.

"Just get it," said my mom.

"Fine!" I grabbed my phone and looked.

`I think this was meant for someone else.`

From Nareem.

Huh? I was confused. My first thought was that he'd made the mistake. Then my heart started pounding, and I scrolled up.

`I didn't say I still liked Nareem! I said he was a great boyfriend. LOL! G2G`

My mouth suddenly went really dry. I let out a little gasp and started hyperventilating.

I DIDN'T SAY I STILL LIKED NAREEM! I SAID HE WAS A GREAT BOYFRIEND.

LOL!

Oh, no. Oh no oh no oh no oh no oh no!!!!!

I meant to send it to Charlie Joe, but sent it to Nareem instead.

Nareem—the absolute nicest, most caring person in the whole world.

I immediately felt like the smallest, lowest person in the whole world.

I felt like dying.

Tears sprang to my eyes. I covered my face with a pillow. "Noooooooo!"

My parents ran over to me, asking questions. "What is it, honey?" "What's going on?" "Can we help?"

But I didn't answer. I just kept crying. Finally I managed to croak out, "Please just leave me alone."

My mom looked scared. "Please tell us what's happening, honey."

"Not right now," I moaned. "Later I will, I promise."

My parents looked at each other, then came to a silent decision.

"Okay, sweetheart," my dad whispered to me gently. "We'll be back in a little while."

"A very little while," I heard my mom whisper to my dad, as they slipped out of the room.

I turned all the lights off in my room and lay down on my bed for hours. My breathing slowly returned to normal. My parents came back every few minutes, but I couldn't talk to them. Finally, I started to calm down, as my horror turned to sadness, and embarrassment, and then complete exhaustion.

I wrote the lyrics to my first song.

Then I cried myself to sleep.

I didn't know it at the time, but I had just sent my last text.

11

HOW

HOW?
Lyrics by Katie Friedman
(Music not written yet)

How do you
Speak the words
That you never thought would be spoken?

How do you
Break the heart
That never has been broken?

How do you
Find the strength
To finally walk out the door?

How do you
Tell the one you loved
You don't love them anymore?

I want to know.
I need to know.
I have to know right now.
I'm on my knees
So someone please
Please come show me how.

How do you
Look someone in the eye
When you're not sure what you want to see?

How do you
Say the words
There is no more you and me?

How do you
Resist the urge
To hide behind a screen?

How do you
Know it's time
To give up the machine?

I want to know.
I need to know.
I have to know right now.
I'm on my knees
So someone please
Please come show me how.

SOMETHING BEAUTIFUL

I stayed home sick from school the next day.

My parents didn't question me. I think because they're therapists, they know that it's pointless to try to talk to someone, until that person is ready to talk.

As soon as the school day was over, I got on my bicycle and rode over to Nareem's house.

His little sister opened the door.

"Hi, Ru. Is your brother home?"

She looked at me and squinted her eyes. At first I thought she looked mad, but then I realized I was imagining it.

"Hold on a second."

She ran off, and I waited at the door. And I waited. I heard some low voices. I waited some more. After about three minutes, I headed back toward my bike.

"Hello."

I turned around. Nareem was at the door. He was

shielding his eyes with his hands, like he was protecting himself from a bright sun. But it was a cloudy morning. I think it was just his way of making sure he didn't look directly at me.

"Hi." I stood there, not sure which direction to go.

"You can come in if you want."

Nareem went back inside, and I followed. He headed to the kitchen, where his parents stood.

"Hi, Mr. and Mrs. Ramdal."

They both nodded. Neither one spoke.

Nareem went to the fridge. "Can I offer you something to drink?" Still not looking at me.

"Nareem, I—" My eyes darted to his parents.

I think I saw a tiny look of pity cross Mr. Ramdal's face. "We will leave you two to discuss this privately," he said.

My face went hot as they walked away. "You told them?"

"I do not hide anything from my parents," Nareem said. "Would you like a drink or not."

"Just some water."

He poured me a glass, and we sat at his kitchen table. I had no idea what to say, except for the obvious.

"I'm sorry, Nareem. I'm so, so sorry."

He stared out the window. "I would be curious to know if you have felt this way for a long time."

"What do you mean?"

Nareem's voice was calm and not at all angry.

"Obviously I now realize that this is what you wished to talk to me about in study hall last week," Nareem said. "And it is equally obvious that you changed your mind after I told you about the Plain Jane concert."

I felt my body fill with shame.

"You're right," I whispered. "But I was torn about it. I like you so much. I didn't know what to do. I would never ever do anything to hurt you—"

"But you have hurt me. LOL, you wrote. I didn't know there was meanness in you like that."

There was nothing to say to that. So I said nothing.

"You have come to apologize in person. That is brave." He looked at me for the first time. "You could have texted, after all."

I felt the need to cry, but I stopped myself. "You're so mad at me," I said. "You're so mad at me." I reached into my pocket and pulled out a crumpled piece of paper. "I wrote a song. About us. About the truth. I don't think we should be boyfriend and girlfriend anymore. But you are still the most amazing person I think I've ever met."

He walked over to the table, hesitated, and picked up the piece of paper. He read it. For the first time, I saw the sadness in his face. And then he smiled.

"You have written something beautiful."

And then I did cry.

NAREEM

Nareem and I talked for two more hours.

I told him again that the last thing I ever wanted to do was hurt him. I told him that I didn't want to be a therapist anymore; I wanted to be a musician. I told him I didn't know how I felt about Charlie Joe, but that I thought I might want to find out. I told him that my parents never kissed each other in front of me.

I told him things I had never told anyone else before.

He told me that the night I first kissed him at Camp Rituhbukkee was the best night of his life, but that when he saw me hug Charlie Joe on the last day of camp, he thought that one day Charlie Joe and I would become boyfriend and girlfriend. He told me that his dream in life was to dunk a basketball.

We talked more that day than we had in nine months of going out, until finally I got up from the kitchen table where we'd been sitting. "I should go. Thank you again for letting me come over and talk to you. I'm so grateful."

Nareem got up, too, and picked up the piece of paper with my lyrics on it. "Your song."

I looked at him nervously. "You really like it?"

He stared at the paper. I couldn't tell if he was reading or thinking. Finally, he put it back on the table.

"I'll have my father send it to Jane."

It took me a minute to understand what he was saying. "Jane? Plantero? Plain Jane?"

Nareem nodded. "Yes. The other night, she asked you to write a song and send it to her. It's an amazing opportunity, and it would be foolish to let it go to waste."

I stood there, unable to move. "Nareem, I don't know what to say—"

"If you write her a note and give it to me, I'll have my father send it to her tomorrow."

Suddenly, I was hugging him. There was a lot in that hug. Guilt, sadness, regret, gratitude, pain, joy.

"Bring me the note in a sealed envelope," he said softly. "I don't want to be tempted to read it."

"Why are you being so nice to me?" I mumbled into his shoulder.

"I am just being me," he answered.

I kept hugging until Nareem gently pulled away. Then I cried a few last tears. "Thank you," I said. "For everything. Thank you."

"You're welcome," Nareem said.

As I biked home, I thought about what had just happened. And I realized something. I was shocked, I was amazed, but I wasn't surprised. Because of where the kindness and generosity came from.

That was Nareem.

14

THE LETTER

Dear Jane,

    The concert was so amazing the other night. And meeting you was definitely the most amazing part of all.

    I have been thinking a lot about what you said about communicating with people and not being so dependent on phones and other devices. I think you're definitely right. I really learned that the other night when I made a terrible mistake and hurt someone I really care about in a text. I feel unbelievably horrible. Texting and IM-ing and stuff can be really dangerous, and it seems like people are using it too much instead of doing things like talking to each other, and it can make people insensitive and mean.

I don't know if you meant it or not when you said to send you a song, but I decided to write one anyway. It felt good to write it. So far it's just lyrics. Here it is. I really hope you like it.

Your biggest fan,

Katie Friedman

SOMETIMES IT TAKES A LITTLE SADNESS

Two nights later, I was eating dinner with my parents when our home phone rang.

My mom and dad looked at each other, since no one ever really called the house except for people trying to sell us stuff. In fact, my parents had been talking recently about getting rid of the home phone altogether.

I got up to look at the caller ID. BLOCKED. I hesitated for a second, then picked up the phone. "Hello?"

"Is this Katie?"

"Yes?"

"This is Kit St. Claire."

It took me a minute to process this. *Kit St. Claire?* I remembered meeting a Kit. Then it hit me. *KIT.*

"Kit?"

"Yup. You remember me, right? I work for Jane."

"Oh. Uh . . . Oh, yes. I remember you." It was hard to hear myself—or anything—over the pounding of my heart.

"Do you have a minute to talk with Jane?"

I had a *year* to talk with Jane. "Um . . . Of course! Yes."

"Great! Hold on a sec."

As I waited, my parents looked at me with puzzled expressions on their faces. I'd told them about meeting Jane backstage, but nothing about her asking me to write a song and send it to her. I hadn't told them about that, because it seemed so ridiculous to think that anything would come from it.

But now, it seemed like something might.

"It's a long story," I whispered to my parents.

"That's okay, we've got time," said my dad.

I rolled my eyes at him and waited. And waited.

And waited some more.

After about two full minutes, with my parents staring at me the whole time, I decided to come clean. "Jane Plantero from Plain Jane is calling me, I think about a song I wrote," I told them, trying to make it sound as normal as possible. "I'm waiting for her to come to the phone."

My parents stared at me. Finally my mom said, "You write songs?"

"I do now, I guess," I said. On the word *guess* I heard a sudden fumbling on the other end of the line, a familiar

65

voice yelling, "Not if I can help it!" at someone, and then a huge, quick laugh.

It was definitely her—Jane, of Plain Jane.

On the phone.

Calling me.

If only life were recorded, I would play that moment over and over and over again.

"Hey, Flattery Girl, what's going on?"

"Um . . . Well, I can't believe you're calling me."

Another loud, rock-and-roll laugh. "Yeah, well, here I am!"

I tried to laugh too, but I think I was hyperventilating, so I'm not sure any noise came out.

"Katie, I have a question for you. Did you really write those lyrics Pops Ramdal sent me?"

I nodded, but then realized you can't hear a nod over the phone, so I said, "Yeah."

"Well, they're good," said my favorite songwriter ever. "They're really good." Then she yelled off the phone, "Right, Kit?" Then back to me: "Kit thinks so, too."

"This is unbelievable," I said.

Jane laughed again, and said, "Yup, it is kind of unbelievable. I was reading this song, and I was thinking about this girl in middle school, feeling these intense feelings, feeling a little trapped by them, and not quite knowing what to do with them, and then finally realizing that writing is the way out. Writing is freedom."

I was shocked that she could get inside my head so accurately. "Wow," I said. "That's amazing. You totally know exactly how I was feeling."

Jane laughed softly. "I wasn't talking about you," she said. "I was talking about me."

Neither of us spoke for a few seconds after that.

"Well, I *was* feeling sad," I said, finally. "When I wrote it, I mean."

"Ah. Well, sometimes it takes a little sadness to let the art out."

I nodded again, but this time I felt she knew I was nodding, so I didn't say anything.

"So listen, sweetie," Jane continued. "We're taking a break from the road, and I've got a little time on my hands. So how would you like to come down to my studio tomorrow afternoon and have a look around? We'll talk about these lyrics of yours, figure out how to turn it into a real song. You game?"

You know how you have the moment when you say to yourself, "My life is changing forever, right now," but you don't really believe it, or you don't really trust it, even though you're hearing it with your own two ears?

I was having that moment.

"I would absolutely love to come to your studio," I somehow managed to say into the phone. I glanced at my parents, whose eyes were going wide. "I would be totally honored."

"Great! I gotta run, so I'm going to put Kit back on the phone. She'll talk it over with your folks, work everything out. Sound like a plan?"

"Absolutely," I said. "Thank you so, so much!"

Jane laughed again. "No, thank *you*," she said. "The world needs people who can write. Turns out you're one of 'em. It's a gift, and I'm here to make sure you don't waste it. See you tomorrow."

"See you tomorrow," I said, but she was already gone.

I handed the phone to my mom and sat down at the kitchen table, trying to get a handle on the most amazing five minutes of my life. One thing kept running through my head: This fantastic thing that was happening to me was all because of a boy whose heart I had just broken.

Life is really weird sometimes.

TWO PELICANS

I knew I was in a different world when we drove through the gates at Jane's house and the first thing I saw was a huge marble statue of two pelicans playing guitar.

"What on earth is that?" said my mom.

"Two pelicans playing guitar," I answered.

She looked at me. "Thanks for clearing that up."

We were met at the door by some guy who introduced himself as Nigel. He had an English accent and hair down to his butt.

"Jane's in the Plastic Room," Nigel said.

My mom and I looked at each other.

"It's a room with a lot of plastic in it," Nigel explained.

"Oh," we said.

And off we went to the Plastic Room, which was filled with giant plastic chairs, couches, and tables. They were all brightly colored and incredibly shiny. It felt like what a room might look like in a four-year-old's dream.

Jane was on an orange couch, with her eyes closed, wearing a pair of headphones the size of a small country. She was swaying slightly back and forth, moving to the beat of something. She had no idea we were standing two feet in front of her.

My mom and I looked at Nigel. "Give her a minute," he said.

Approximately eight minutes later, the song ended and Jane opened her eyes. She saw us standing there and broke into a big smile.

"Yo!" she hollered, whipping off her headphones and leaping up from the orange plastic couch. She hugged me, then hugged my mom. "Welcome to Two Pelicans!"

"Thank you," said my mom. "Now, about the pelican thing—"

"I *love* pelicans," Jane said. "Always have. Was obsessed with them as a kid. They are the most awesome-looking creatures. I would have pet pelicans but this environment is just all wrong." Jane gestured around the room. "You like the Plastic Room?"

"I've been meaning to ask you about that, too," said my mom.

Jane knocked her hand against the table. "Plastic! Ugh! The hardest material to get rid of. Doesn't decompose. Just sits there taking up valuable earth space. So I decided to start collecting plastic and making good use of it. I got a whole company now dedicated to collecting plastic and making furniture. It's actually doing really well."

"That is so amazing," I said. "You are so amazing."

Jane laughed her big laugh. "Cut it out, Flattery Girl! I just got lucky. But you know something? I got lucky because I worked hard. And I believed in myself. So, yeah. How's that for a segue?"

"What's a *seg-way*?" I asked.

"A segue," Jane explained, "is a way to go smoothly from one song to another. Or one topic to another. And I want to go from the topic of me to the topic of you." She looked at Nigel. "Is the Black Room ready?"

"Ready," Nigel confirmed.

Jane turned back to us. "Let's go."

We followed her down a long hall, around a corner, out

71

a door, across a stone path, through a cottage filled with manufactured pelicans of all shapes and sizes, and finally, into a giant barn that was completely dark except for one red light blinking on the far wall.

"Hold on a sec." Jane disappeared into the darkness. Suddenly there was a sharp click, and dim light filled the room. Everything was black—the walls, the couches, the carpeting, even the huge refrigerator in the corner.

"Can I ask why you call it the Black Room?" my mom asked.

Jane roared with laughter. "Holy smokes, Katie, your mom is a funny girl!"

But I wasn't paying attention. I was staring. Because the room was filled with more instruments and musical equipment than I thought existed in the world. Guitars, basses, keyboards, amps, mikes, a beautiful grand piano. All completely black.

"Wow," I whispered.

"Help yourself," Jane said. I looked at her, confused, so she clarified. "Play anything you want."

I think that was the moment my eyes bugged out of my head.

"I can't."

Jane walked over to a completely gorgeous pitch-black Gibson Les Paul guitar, picked it up, and put it in my hand. "Can't isn't an option," she said.

I didn't know what to say, so I just stared down at the guitar. Then I played one chord—E major. It sounded like the most perfect chord ever.

"Jane, you are being so incredibly kind to my daughter," my mom said, sitting down on one of the black couches. "Do you mind if I ask you one question?"

"Shoot," said Jane.

My mom thought for a second, then said, simply, "Why?"

"Jane's from Eastport," I reminded my mom, as if that answered the question.

Jane plopped down onto the rolling chair behind the massive soundboard. She started rolling back and forth, playing with knobs.

"Katie, did you show your parents the lyrics you sent me?" asked Jane.

"No," I said quickly.

"Why not?"

"I don't know."

"Do you mind if I show it to her?"

I glanced at my mom. "I guess not."

Jane pushed a button and my lyrics came up on a huge screen hanging from the ceiling (which was black, btw).

I looked at them and suddenly felt terribly embarrassed.

How do you
Speak the words
That you never thought would be spoken?

How do you
Break the heart
That never has been broken?

I watched my mom as she read the lyrics. Her face looked like a combination of shock, concern, and pride.

Afterward, she looked at me. "Now I get it," she said. "Now it makes sense."

Jane's eyes went back and forth between my mom and me. "What does?"

I jumped in. "My parents have been telling me that I text too much, that I IM too much, Instagram, Snapchat, all that stuff," I said.

"Sounds familiar," Jane said, smiling.

"Yeah," I said. "We fight about it a lot. I always told them they were crazy. But then something really bad happened."

I stopped for a second and looked up at the screen again.

How do you
Look someone in the eye
When you're not sure what you want to see?

How do you
Say the words
There is no more you and me?

"Mr. Ramdal's son, Nareem, has been my boyfriend for almost a year," I continued, "even though I'd been thinking about breaking up with him for a while. But I was never able to do it. Then I thought about doing it on text. Because you can say a lot of things on text that you're too scared to say in person."

"That's for dang sure," Jane said.

"So I had decided to do it, but then he invited me to your concert, and to meet you and everything, and so of course I couldn't do it. But the night after the concert, I was texting with a bunch of people, my friend Becca who's in my band, and my friend Charlie Joe, and Nareem. And Charlie Joe knew I didn't really like Nareem anymore, and we were joking around about it on text. And I sent a text that said something like 'Well, yeah, I don't like Nareem anymore, but of course I can't break up with him now that he helped me meet Jane,' or something like that."

I paused to take a deep breath. The only sound in the room was the buzzing of all the equipment.

"Only, I sent it to Nareem instead of Charlie Joe."

Jane whistled. "Holy—." Thankfully she remembered she was with a girl and her mother, and she stopped.

Nigel popped his head in.

"Can I get anyone a juice or a coffee?"

"Mango soy juice all around," Jane said. *Ew*, I thought to myself. Nigel nodded and disappeared.

Jane got up and went to the piano. She casually played a few of the most beautiful chords I'd ever heard. Then she stopped and looked at me.

"Your mom asked why I'm being so nice to you," Jane said. "It's because you're me. You're me! Don't you get it?"

"Not really," I said.

"I was just like you!" Jane said. "I wanted to write, but I was too shy, too insecure, too nervous. But I made myself do it! I made myself!" Then she pointed at the guitar in my hands. "I want you to finish the song."

"Now?"

Jane hooted. "No, not now, silly."

I stared down at the guitar. "You mean write the music?"

Jane nodded. "I mean, write the song. Make it a complete thing. Finish what you started."

I tried to imagine coming up with chords and a melody to the words I'd written.

"I don't know if I can."

"Of course you can," Jane said.

For some reason, her being so confident in me made me way less confident in myself. "I'm really busy," I said, lamely.

"Oh, please. Doing what? Sending texts and photos to your friends? That's another reason why that stuff is so dangerous—it's killing creativity! If I had Facebook and Twitter and texting and all that stuff to distract me, I don't know if I ever would have written even one song."

Nigel knocked and brought in a big tray of snacks and drinks.

"I would love to give up all that stuff," I heard myself say. "It would make life so much easier."

Jane directed her blazing eyes right at me. "So why don't you?"

I wasn't sure I understood what she meant. "Why don't I what?"

"Give up your phone," Jane said. She got up and started pacing around the room. She looked like she was getting more and more excited about the possibility. "Just try it! See how it feels!"

Yikes. Was she serious?

"Um, I don't know," I mumbled. "That's kind of impossible. I need my phone just to deal with everyday life, with everything going on."

"You don't! Trust me, you don't."

I looked up at her. "I don't?"

"I don't text," Jane said. "I don't IM. I don't do Facebook or Twitter. Now it's true, I do have an online profile, which Kit keeps up for me, but it's just business. But personally, I refuse to be defined by that stuff, because it's no way to live. It makes us mean, and it wastes our time, and it prevents us from being real people." She pointed at the screen. "It stops us from doing the writing that really matters."

I tried to process everything Jane was saying. *No texting? No Facebook?*

Holy moly.

"You can do this," she continued, really getting into the idea. "Give up your phone, texting, all that stuff. It would be so awesome. Your friends could to it, too." Suddenly she clapped her hands together. "How about this? I'll make a deal with you!"

"What kind of deal?"

"You and ten of your friends give up your phones for one week."

I sighed and laughed at the same time. "That will never happen."

"Why not?"

"You haven't met my friends."

Jane picked up a different guitar and started tuning it. "Okay, I'll sweeten the pot," she said. "If you give up your phone for a week, and get ten friends to give up theirs, too, I will get all of you backstage passes to a show. *And* I'll bring you guys up on stage."

Then she pointed up at my lyrics.

"And we'll play your song," Jane said.

My eyes bugged out of my head. *Play my song?!*

"In front of everybody?" I asked.

Jane's eyes twinkled. "In front of everybody. If you finish it, that is."

I felt my jaw drop open. For about the fiftieth time in the last couple of days, I was too shocked to speak.

"But here's the thing," Jane added. "You can't tell your friends that you came here today. They can't know about our deal, or anything about my playing your song or inviting them on stage. I don't want them eating the Cracker Jacks just because there's a prize in the box."

I didn't know what that meant, but I was too hyped up to care. Instead I asked, "So how am I going to get them to give up their phones?"

"That's for you to figure out," Jane said.

I looked over at my mom. She was talking to Nigel and had missed this whole part of the conversation, which was fine by me.

"How are you going to know that we really did it?" I asked Jane. "I could just tell you we did, even if we don't."

"I trust you," Jane said.

"Why would you trust me?"

Jane laughed. "I have keen powers of observation. I guess that's what makes me a decent songwriter."

And that was it. I was all out of questions.

Jane stuck out her hand. "What do you say?" she said. "Do we have a deal?

We had a deal.

After we shook hands on it, Jane turned around and grabbed another guitar and handed it to me. "Now let's make some music."

For the next half hour, we jammed. That's right, *I jammed with Jane Plantero*. We played three Beatles songs, a Stones song, a Joan Jett song, and a Patti Smith song. No Plain Jane songs, though: "That's the last thing I want to hear right now," Jane said.

We didn't stop until Nigel stuck his head in and said two words: "Satellite interview." Jane put down her guitar, hugged me, and said, "One week. No phones. You can do it. Can't wait to hear the song."

Then she was gone.

As my mom and I drove back out through the gates and headed home, I stared at the huge statue of the guitar-playing pelicans.

Jane was right, I thought—they really are amazing-looking creatures.

Part 2
THE SAME, ONLY DIFFERENT.

A NOT-SO-BUSY MORNING

Here's what happened *before* breakfast on Monday, April 30:

I woke up, showered, brushed my teeth, and got dressed.

Here's what happened *during* breakfast on Monday, April 30:

I ate cereal and talked with my parents.

In the middle of our conversation, my mom suddenly realized something. "Where's your phone?" she asked. "Why aren't you texting your friends?"

"Don't feel like it," I answered, shrugging.

Here's what happened on the bus ride to school on Monday, April 30:

I read a book.

18

CHARLIE JOE JACKSON'S GUIDE TO WHY TEXTING IS AWESOME

Charlie Joe was the first one to notice. He cornered me at school, just before lunch.

"Why aren't you returning any of my texts?"

"I don't know, just haven't gotten around to it, I guess."

"Nobody doesn't get around to texting," he said. I wasn't sure that was proper English, but I knew what he meant.

"Well, I didn't," I said. "I'm giving up texting for a while, and Instagram, and all that stuff because it was starting to control my life and dominate my thoughts."

"You say that like it's a bad thing," Charlie Joe said.

I smacked him on the arm. "It *is* a bad thing. You just have your nose buried too far into your phone to notice."

"This thing changed my life," Charlie Joe said, holding up his cell phone. "Now I can send seven-word texts instead of getting into long, boring conversations with people. Get in, get out, that's what I say." Right on cue, his phone beeped. He checked it and laughed. "See that? Timmy, texting me that Sheila's hairnet is on backward today."

I glared at him. Sheila is one of our lunch ladies and one of the sweetest people you'll ever meet.

"See, that's what I mean," I said. "Who cares about Sheila's hairnet? It's just another opportunity for you to make fun of someone behind their back."

Charlie Joe looked annoyed. "Hold on a second. Come with me." He took my hand and dragged me over to the lunch line, where Sheila was slicing pizza. "Hey, Sheila," Charlie Joe called. "Do you know your hairnet is on backward? It looks kind of goofy."

Sheila laughed. "Yeah, well, that's pretty funny coming from a kid who never manages to wear matching socks."

"That's not true," Charlie Joe protested. "I wore matching socks two Thursdays ago."

"Well, I'll be sure to alert the newspapers," Sheila said, still chuckling.

Charlie Joe pretended to be confused. "What's a newspaper? Oh yeah, those weird things with writing on them, for old people like you."

"HA!" Sheila gave Charlie Joe a little pat on the cheek. "Thanks for giving me a laugh every day, you little rascal."

As Sheila went back to her pizza, Charlie Joe and I walked back to our table. "See?" he said. "We make fun of each other all the time. That's what people do. You're overreacting. Having a phone is an essential part of the middle school experience."

I rolled my eyes, mainly because I knew he liked it when I did. We ate quietly for another minute, then I whispered, "Nareem and I broke up."

Charlie Joe dropped his fork. "Huh? When?"

"Over the weekend."

"That's crazy," Charlie Joe said. "What about the concert? And the backstage passes and meeting Jane?"

I lowered my voice even further. "I sent Nareem a text that I meant to send to you. It was awful. He forgave me, because he's an amazing person. But we're not going out anymore."

"Oh, wow." Charlie Joe whistled. "Holy moly. Now I

get the whole text thing." He put his hand on my shoulder. "I'm really sorry."

"It's okay," I said. "It had to happen. Just not this way." I pointed at his phone. "So you go ahead and send all the texts you want. I'm taking a break."

"Got it," Charlie Joe said. Then, after a second, he asked, "Do you mind if I ask you what was in the text you sent to Nareem that you were supposed to send to me?"

"Go put on a pair of matching socks," I answered.

HALLWAY CONVERSATION

I needed to tell two other people about my plan.

Nareem was first. I found him after lunch, walking to Social Studies alone. I slid up alongside him.

"Can I talk to you for a second?"

He didn't look up. "Yes."

"I wanted you to know something. I am giving up texting. I am giving up all that stuff. It's horrible. It's scary. People write things they don't mean and would never say. I need to change—it took hurting you like this to realize that. I wanted to tell you face-to-face."

Nareem nodded. "Good for you. You are following Jane's advice. Connect." Then he started walking a little faster, just to get away from me, I think. "I hope you will connect very well with your next boyfriend."

I hurried to catch up to him. "Nareem, stop."

He stopped.

"The last thing I would ever want to do was to make you unhappy," I told him. "You're seriously the best person I know."

"It is not necessarily always a good thing, being such a good person," Nareem said. "People don't necessarily want good people as their boyfriends. Perhaps I should try to be a bit less good."

"No!"

He finally looked at me. I suddenly felt embarrassed, and had to turn away.

"So, is this real?" he asked me. "You are giving up texting?"

"And everything else," I said. "I'm giving up my whole phone for a week."

"Well, I will be curious to see how it works out," Nareem said. "There are many times during the day we need our phones for important things, like getting in touch with our parents."

I'd already thought of that, before deciding not to think about that. "I'll figure out another way," I said.

"Well, good luck."

We arrived at his classroom. "Oh, one other thing," Nareem said. "I think it's best if we don't talk to each other for a while."

That felt like a punch to the stomach. A punch that I deserved. "Okay," I said.

He gave me a sad smile and walked into the room. I started to reach into my backpack to see if anyone had texted me, stopped myself, and went to class.

TO BAND OR NOT TO BAND

I found Becca at recess, playing basketball with the boys as usual. I watched her play for about five minutes, then waved and got her attention.

"I need to talk to you."

She ran by. "Can it wait?" she asked. "We're up 12–9."

"It's important."

"Guys! Sub!" she yelled, then came over. "What's up? Is this about the other night?"

We hadn't really talked about the whole songwriting thing since she made it clear she wasn't into it. And it was killing me not to tell her about my visit to Jane's studio, but I'd promised Jane I wouldn't. So instead I said, "Well, no, but since you brought it up, I should tell you that I've actually started writing a song."

"That's awesome!"

"It'd be more awesome if you wrote it with me," I added.

I'm not really sure why I said that. I think I was just scared at the idea of writing by myself.

Becca wiped some sweat from her forehead. "Katie, being in a band with you is fun, it really is, but I'm not as into being a musician as you. I'm just not, sorry. I'm not doing it to get famous. It's just supposed to be a fun way to hang out together."

"I'm not doing it to get famous, either, Bec," I said, defensively.

"Okay, sorry, forget it," Becca said. "And I'm sorry if you're mad about band practice."

"What about band practice?"

"I told you I couldn't rehearse again until Friday night."

Now I *was* mad. "Wait, what? Friday night? That's the night before the talent show? What about Wednesday? We practice every Wednesday!"

"I have a playoff game," Becca said. "Like I told you."

"No, you didn't tell me," I said, getting more annoyed.

Becca frowned. "I did. Didn't you get my text?"

Ah, so *that* was it. "No." I pulled Becca over to the jungle gym and took a deep breath. "Actually, that's what I wanted to talk to you about. I'm not using my cell phone anymore."

"What are you talking about?"

"I'm not using my phone. At all! I gave it up."

Becca shook her head. "I don't understand. That doesn't make any sense. Why would you do that?"

"I was getting addicted to it, and I just felt like it was taking over my life."

Becca took out her own phone and stared down at it. "I guess I know what you mean." Then she read a text, laughed, and sent a quick reply. "Oops," she said, looking up at me. "Sorry."

"No, it's fine," I said. I wasn't ready to ask my friends to give up their phones, too. Mainly because I had no idea how I was going to get them to do it.

Becca looked out onto the basketball court. She really wanted to go back in, I could tell.

"So anyway, that's it," I said. "Go ahead back to your game. I'm bummed out about the rehearsal thing, but we'll just have to deal with it."

"It's just a talent show, Katie," Becca said. "It's not a TV show."

She ran back onto the court. As I watched her play, I realized that she was happiest with a ball in her hand, kind of like the way I was happiest with a guitar in my hand. She was in the band because she was my friend, not because she wanted to write songs and change the world.

I suddenly felt selfish that I was trying to force her and the rest of the band to be more like me. It was totally fine to just play famous songs. Lots of bands do. Our band could, too.

I just wasn't sure I wanted to be a part of it.

ELIZA DECIDES TO SAVE HER BRAIN

So now I had to figure out how to get ten of my friends to give up their phones for a week.

Good luck with *that*.

The first thing I did was make a list of the kids I was going to ask. I started with my band: Becca, Sammie, and Jackie. Then I added Charlie Joe, Hannah, Jake, Timmy, Phil, and Celia. I thought about Pete Milano, then crossed him off the list—too much trouble.

But how was I going to convince them? And who would be my tenth person?

I was thinking it over in the locker room after gym when Eliza Collins sashayed by, looking at herself in the mirror as usual.

"Hey, Eliza," I said.

She barely glanced at me. "Do my shoulders look fat in this shirt?"

That gave me an idea.

I can't remember, but I might have mentioned that Eliza is the acknowledged great beauty of our school. And much as I might have wanted to, I couldn't argue with that assessment. She was gorgeous, no doubt about it. She was so pretty that she'd spent the previous summer modeling in Spain, and rumor had it she'd had lunch with Jonah Hill while he was shooting a movie there. So that made her officially personal-relationship-with-a-movie-star pretty.

Here's the not-so-secret secret about pretty girls in middle school: People tend to pay attention to them and do what they do. When the pretty girl starts playing volleyball at recess, other kids start playing volleyball at recess. When the pretty girl decides to join the walk against breast cancer, other kids decide to join the walk against breast cancer.

And when the pretty girl decides to give up her phone for a week, other kids will decide to give up their phones for a week.

"No, your shoulders don't look fat in that shirt," I told her.

Right on cue, she pulled out her phone and fired off a text.

I glanced around. "You're not supposed to text in the locker room."

"Who cares?"

Oh, to have the confidence of a gorgeous person.

"Eliza," I asked her, "how many texts a day do you think you send?"

She didn't look up from her phone. "What?"

"How many texts a day do you send?"

She still didn't look up, but she frowned. "I don't know and I don't care. Why?"

"Because it could hurt your brain."

She looked up in alarm. "WHAT?!"

Here's the more-secret secret about pretty girls in middle school: The only thing they ever really worry about is people thinking they're not smart. And they're right: Most of the regular-looking kids assume that the really good-looking kids can't be intelligent. I think because it's impossible to admit that attractive people can also be really smart. That would just be too unfair to take.

Which is where my idea came in.

"It's true," I said. "Don't you remember the study that Ms. Kransky was talking about in class the other day?"

This was the great thing about my idea: I wasn't totally making it up. Ms. Kransky really had been talking about a study that reported on teenagers' increased usage of cell phones.

"What about it?" Eliza asked.

"Well, apparently kids who send more than one hundred text messages a day are burning brain cells at an alarming rate."

This got her to actually stop looking at her phone. "Is that true?"

It wasn't, entirely, but I nodded anyway. "Not only that, it said that people are becoming so addicted to their phones that over 50 percent of today's middle school kids may become technically brain-dead by the age of thirty-five."

Eliza's eyes bugged out of her head. "No way!"

This is the part where I should probably tell you that even though pretty girls worry a lot about other kids not thinking they're smart, that doesn't necessarily mean that they're all that smart in the first place.

I nodded gravely. "Way."

Eliza immediately put her phone in her pocket like it had cooties.

"That's like, horrible!"

I suddenly felt a little guilty. But not that guilty. "I know. I feel like it's up to us to do something about it. Don't you?"

Eliza had returned to the mirror, but that didn't mean she wasn't listening. "Like what?"

I grabbed her hand conspiratorially. "I was thinking about giving up my cell phone for a week. Just to see if I could do it. But it would be even better if you did it, too! And if we got some other kids to do it with us! We could become famous as the kids who saved other kids from cell phone addiction and preserved people's brain cells!"

This is the last total generalization I'll make about pretty middle school girls, I swear: They all want to be famous, and think they probably will be, since they're already famous in middle school.

And Eliza was halfway there already, since she'd already modeled in Spain.

"How famous?" Eliza asked, already thinking about the possibilities.

"I bet we could get on TV," I answered, thinking that would pretty much seal the deal.

But Eliza wasn't quite sold. "What about all my friends? How will they reach me? And what will we do at night and stuff?"

I was ready for that one. "Well, what's better than knowing someone is trying to text you, but them thinking you're too busy to text them back?"

I could see the wheels turning in Eliza's head. The idea of giving up her phone was frightening, but hopefully, becoming famous and having people desperately but unsuccessfully trying to reach you would more than make up for it.

Finally she turned to me. "Are you sure my shoulders don't look fat in this shirt?"

"Positive," I nodded.

"Thank God," Eliza said, taking a deep breath. She walked toward the locker room door, ready to resume her place at the head of the middle school food chain. I was beginning to think that our whole conversation had been for nothing, when she turned back and squinted at me.

"So you think that all we have to do is give up our phones for one week, and then we can use them for the rest of our lives, and our brain cells will be saved?"

Hmm. That was a tough one. I decided to keep my answer simple.

"Yes," I said. "Yes, I do."

Eliza paused for a second, then said, "Exactly how stupid do you think I am?"

Oops. So forget all the stereotypes I just talked about.

Then she laughed, took out her cell phone, and handed it to me. "This could be fun anyway," she said. "I'm kind of into the idea of being suddenly and completely unreachable. People are going to totally freak out."

"They totally are!" I agreed, feeling really dumb for just assuming Eliza was really dumb.

She flipped her hair and pointed at her phone, which was now in my hand. "If Brian texts, tell him I'm eating lunch with Ricky," she said, getting into the spirit right away.

22

SAVE OUR BRAINS WEEK!

Pretty soon—as in, approximately two and a half minutes—word got around school that Eliza Collins and her new best friend Katie Friedman had decided to give up their cell phones for a week.

Then something amazing happened during lunch: I realized I wouldn't have to ask anyone else to give up their phones.

What happened was this: Eliza was eating lunch with Ricky, one table over from me. I overheard Eliza say to him, "And I don't want to kill my brain cells, which is why I decided to give up my phone." Then I heard Ricky say back to her, "Well, I don't want to kill my brain cells either, so I'm going to give up my phone, too!"

"Whatever," Eliza said.

Immediately Ricky got up and came over to me and

handed me his phone. "I hear you're the one collecting phones for Save Our Brains Week. I'm in."

Suddenly I understood—that was it! If you beg kids to give up their phones, they won't do it. But if they think it's just this weird, cool thing you're doing with a friend or two, they'll want in.

Charlie Joe, Timmy, Jake, Hannah, Phil, and Celia were all sitting at my table, eavesdropping on Eliza's conversation, too. Charlie Joe smirked. "Save Our Brains Week?"

"It's a known fact that overuse of cell phones can hurt your brain," I said.

"I'm not so sure about that," Jake said. Considering he used his phone all the time and was a complete genius, he made a pretty convincing point.

"Listen, you guys can believe me or not," I said. "This is just something I've decided to do. To tell you the truth, it's less about my brain and more just wanting to know if I can live without something I've depended on for so long."

Hannah looked at Jake, who happened to be her boyfriend. "Hmm. That sounds like an interesting experiment."

"Interesting how?" Jake asked. "Yeah, people overuse their phones sometimes; I'm as guilty as anyone else. But the idea of giving them up is ridiculous. How would we look up our homework assignments from the car? How would we get in touch with our parents? How would they get in touch with us?"

"Ah," said Charlie Joe. "That's an excellent question. If Jake's mom couldn't get in touch with him every ten minutes, I think her head might explode."

"That's hilarious, Charlie Joe," Jake said.

"Mommy Katz would not be happy," Timmy added, as if anyone missed Charlie Joe's point.

Jake threw his phone on the table. "Fine. You guys don't think I can give up my phone for a week? Here, take it."

Hannah's eyes went wide. "Seriously?"

"Yup." Jake snickered. "Sounds like a fun game. Let's play."

"Trust me dude, you're going to love not hearing from your mom for a week," Charlie Joe said.

Hannah smiled at Jake, then pulled out her phone, too. "Well, if you're going to save your brain, I'm going to save mine, too."

Phil and Celia stared in shock. "Are you guys serious?

You're giving up your phones? For a whole WEEK?" They looked at each other, shrugged, then Phil let out a deep breath. "Fine." He put his phone on the table.

Celia did the same two seconds later. "What am I going to do without Snapchat?" she asked sadly.

"Not send pictures of yourself every three minutes?" I said.

"Ha-ha-ha," she said.

That left Charlie Joe and Timmy. We all looked at them and waited.

"What?" Charlie Joe said.

"Yeah, what?" Timmy echoed.

"Nothing," we said.

Charlie Joe shook his head. "I'm not giving you people my phone, if that's what you're wondering."

Timmy looked relieved. "And neither am I."

"Cell phones are for losers," Jake said.

Charlie Joe laughed.

"Well then, I lose," he said.

PEGGY CHANGES
HER MIND

By the time lunch was over, ten people had given
me their phones:

> Eliza
> Ricky
> Tiffany (an Elizette)
> Amber (an Elizette)
> Hannah
> Jake
> Phil
> Celia
> Becca
> Jackie

The last two joined in when I was leaving lunch and I saw

Becca, Jackie, and Sammie—my bandmates—sitting at a table by the juice machines.

I happened to walk by them—on purpose, of course.

"Hey, what's this about you giving up your phone for a week?" Becca shouted.

"Oh, that," I said. "It's no big deal. Just something I'm doing with Eliza."

Sammie snorted. "Eliza?" I kind of knew she would react that way. Sammie had never been a huge fan of Eliza's. Probably because Eliza had called her "Peggy" all through third grade—short for "Peggy Penguin"—because Sammie happened to walk with her feet pointed out a little bit.

Girls have long memories when it comes to insults like that.

"Yup," I said. "It's just something we decided during gym, to see if we could do it, you know? And now a bunch of other kids are doing it, too."

Becca stopped chewing. "Hold on a second. You told me you were giving up texting. Now all of a sudden you're giving up your whole phone for a week? And so are a bunch of other kids?" She looked at me like she thought I was up to something. "What's this about?"

Eliza came up behind me. "It's not about anything," she said. "We just don't want our brains to die. Is that so wrong?"

"Absolutely not," Jackie said, trying not to laugh. "Brains should definitely not die."

Becca stood up. "Well, I'm always up for something new and different," she said, putting her phone on the table. "Take it," she said to me. I took it and put it in my backpack.

Jackie and Sammie looked at each other. I could tell neither one wanted to give up their phones, but there's that moment in every middle school kid's life where they worry if they don't go along with what everyone else is doing, they're going to be left behind forever.

"What the hey," Jackie said, handing me her phone, but Sammie hesitated.

"My mom is supposed to text me what time she's picking me up after school," Sammie said.

"There are a ton of kids who still have their phones," Eliza said. "Just use one of theirs."

"Oh, right," Sammie said, a little embarrassed that the girl who was worried about her brain dying had an idea that she hadn't thought of. She handed me her phone.

"Thanks, Peggy Penguin," Eliza said.

Sammie grabbed her phone back. "Forget it, you little blond twerp."

Eliza walked away, smiling. Sammie sat there, seething.

Old habits die hard, I guess.

MS. KRANSKY

Ms. Kransky, my language arts teacher, was one of my favorites, because you could tell she wasn't just counting the years until retirement. Not that I blame teachers who do that by the way—have *you* ever tried convincing a bunch of middle schoolers that learning is a good thing? It can't be easy.

But Ms. Kransky was different. She seemed to really care about making a difference in kids' lives. She had definitely made a difference in mine, starting with the time she told me that poetry didn't have to rhyme. That was a major breakthrough. Although song lyrics do have to rhyme. That's a rule that even my dad's favorite singer, Bob Dylan, wouldn't break.

And there was one other thing about Ms. Kransky: She *hated* cell phones. She claimed she didn't even own one.

She was always complaining about how cell phones and Twitter and Instagram were ruining the lives of young Americans.

Which is why I wanted to talk to her.

I got to class a few minutes early, when she was grading papers.

"Ms. Kransky? Can I talk to you for a second?"

She looked up at me and took off her glasses. "Time's up."

I wasn't sure if she was kidding, but I laughed, just to be safe. Then I pointed at my backpack. "You'll never guess what I have in here."

She smiled tiredly. "I don't really have time to guess, Katie."

"Oh, right." I reached into the backpack and took out as many phones as I could hold, which was about five. "Ten kids' cell phones."

Ms. Kransky squinted her eyes. "And why do you have these phones?"

"A bunch of us thought that we were becoming dangerously addicted to our phones, so we decided to give them up for a week, just to see if we could do it."

Ms. Kransky's eyes went wide, then she did something I've never seen her do to any student before.

She gave me a hug.

"Katie, you are something else! A true leader!"

I felt proud, but also a little phony, since the real reason

I was doing it was because I insulted Nareem by accident, and Jane promised to sing my song. And the only reason other kids joined in was because Eliza is so pretty.

But there didn't seem to be any point in dwelling on that stuff right then.

"Thanks," I said, hugging her back. Then I pointed at my backpack. "And also . . . I thought maybe it'd be a good idea if you held on to the phones for us."

"Well, wait just a second," Ms. Kransky said. "I need a little information here. When did this whole thing happen? What if other kids want to join in? I don't want this to become one of those exclusive clubs that people feel bad about if they're not part of it."

Huh. I hadn't thought about that.

"I have an idea!" Ms. Kransky said, before I'd said anything. "What if we make an announcement to the whole class today, that it's a class experiment? All kids are welcome to participate, but those who don't want to can make their own decision."

I was thrilled. "That's a great idea!"

"Great," Ms. Kransky said. "I just need to call everyone's parents first."

Wait a second. "Call everyone's parents?"

Ms. Kransky laughed. "Of course! The school can't authorize taking away a student's personal property without notifying their parents. And some of these kids need their phones for important reasons."

"I thought you hated cell phones!"

"I do," Ms. Kransky said. "But that doesn't mean they're not necessary sometimes. They can come in wonderfully handy. That's the thing with wonderful things. People love them so much that they become addicted to them, and then they go from wonderful to horrible." The class started filing in. "So what do you say? Shall we go for it?"

"Go for *what*?" butted in Charlie Joe, who had just walked into the room. "Does this have anything to do with this crazy no-phone thing?"

I had a decision to make, and I had to make it fast. I decided to keep the phones myself and forget full-class participation. I didn't want to have to deal with Charlie Joe, who was sure to be annoying about the whole thing. And no offense to parents, but I couldn't see how involving them in this experiment could end well.

I stuffed the phones back in my backpack. "Thanks anyway, Ms. Kransky. I'll just hold on to them."

"I still recommend you all tell your parents. Now go—I gave you way more than a second—even way more than a minute. When am I going to get these papers graded now?"

"I'm not sure."

"Well, this should be interesting," she said, her eyes twinkling. "Keep me posted. And good luck."

Part 3
THE PHONIES VERSUS THE CAVEMEN

NOW WHAT?

So it turns out it's really hard to get eleven people together for a meeting, when you don't have phones.

I spent the entire recess running around to everyone who'd given me their phones, arranging a quick meeting after school. There were only about ten minutes between the end of school and bus pickup, so we were going to have to make it quick.

We met at the edge of the blacktop in front of the playground. I saw Charlie Joe, Timmy, and Pete looking at us and pointing.

"Welcome to the beginning of our big experiment," I announced.

"Yes, welcome to all," Eliza repeated. She had decided to be my copilot on this whole thing, and considering she was the one who basically got everyone to give up their phones, I couldn't exactly object.

"The first thing we need to do is figure out where to keep all the phones," I went on. "I asked Ms. Kransky but she said if she took them she would have to tell our parents about this whole thing."

All the kids looked at each another like they hadn't thought about that at all. Which they probably hadn't.

"Why don't you just put them in your locker?" suggested Amber, who was one of Eliza's devoted followers (otherwise known as the Elizettes).

Everyone else nodded.

I frowned. "You guys trust me with your phones?"

Everyone nodded again.

"Okay, I'll store them in my locker and, just to be safe, I won't even use my locker at all for the whole week." This wasn't a big deal, as most kids, including myself, barely ever used their lockers.

"The other thing we wanted to discuss with you guys," Eliza said, "was what we plan on doing for fun, since we don't have our phones. We're going to need some activities and stuff."

Eliza hadn't said a word to me about wanting to discuss this topic, but now that she brought it up, I realized she was absolutely right. What *were* we going to do?

Ricky, Eliza's semi-boyfriend whom I barely knew, raised his hand.

"We should totally party," he said.

"You're too young to use *party* as a verb," Hannah told him. Ricky smirked, but his face turned red.

"You're right, though, we definitely need to have fun things to look forward to so we can make it through the week," Jake said. "We need to do something really fun halfway through, and then something even more fun at the end."

It was hard to argue with someone who had just used the word *fun* three times in two sentences, so we all nodded again.

"I have a question," Phil said. "Does five days count as a week, you know, like a school week? Or does it have to be seven days?

"Good question," said Phil's girlfriend, Celia. "Since today is Monday, can we just say we give up our phones till Friday?"

I thought about that for a second. Jane hadn't been very specific. Technically, of course, a week did mean seven days, but whenever any kid talks about "the week," they're really talking about Monday through Friday.

"Why don't we compromise," I said finally. "Since the talent show is on Saturday night, we'll say that's the end of the week."

More nodding. This was an agreeable bunch. People were so nice to one another face-to-face!

"I can host a barbecue at my house on Wednesday night,"

said Tiffany, another Elizette. "That's kind of the halfway point."

"Great!" I said. "And I bet my parents will let me have a little party after the talent show, to celebrate."

"We can do it!" shouted Becca.

"Yay us!" cheered Celia.

Everyone laughed and cheered and hugged and high-fived. It was like we knew each other so well, like we'd been hanging out forever. It was really kind of cool. It was—

"Weird."

Leave it to Charlie Joe Jackson, who'd wandered over from the jungle gym with Timmy and Pete, to get right to the heart of the matter.

I stared at him. "What's weird?"

Charlie Joe laughed. "What's weird? You want to know what's weird? How about the fact that you and Eliza and the Elizettes are acting like you're besties? And that you guys have to have a meeting to figure out what you're going to do with yourselves since you'll be so bored without your phones. How's that for weird?"

"That's totally beyond weird," Pete chimed in.

"We better go," I said to the group, not even acknowledging Charlie Joe's comment. "See you guys tomorrow."

As we walked to the buses, Charlie Joe slid up next to me.

"What are you doing? What is this all about?"

"I told you already. I was sick of being addicted to my phone. I want to see if I can live without it."

Charlie Joe didn't say anything for a minute. "I don't believe you," he said, finally.

"What do you mean you don't believe me?"

"I mean, I don't believe you."

Charlie Joe stopped walking, and for some reason, I did, too.

"I know you hurt Nareem. I get it," he went on. "But doing this whole phone thing with all these kids? You don't even know half of them. You think the Elizettes are ridiculous, but now you're all pals." He leaned in and whispered, "You're up to something. I know it."

I felt my face go hot. Was there any way he could know about my deal with Jane? I quickly realized it was impossible. "You're being ridiculous. You're the schemer around here, not me."

Charlie Joe laughed that Charlie Joe laugh. "It takes one to know one."

TV NIGHT

"Whatcha watching?"

My parents looked up at me in shock after I asked the question. For good reason. It's probably safe to say that in the past few years, the amount of times I'd wandered into the TV room after dinner to ask them what they were watching was about . . . let's see . . . zero.

It's not that I don't love TV. I do love TV. I just don't love watching it with my parents, when I could be in my room watching it on my computer while texting my friends and sending Snapchat pictures of my dog crossing his legs like a person while lying down. (He's so cute when he does that.)

But that night, I wasn't doing any of those things. Oh sure, I could have been on my computer, since technically, it wasn't off-limits. But I had decided I was going to go all the way. When the week was over, and Jane asked me if I'd been on my computer the whole time, I wanted to be able to say "Absolutely not," and not be lying.

Which brings me to the part where I asked my parents what they were watching.

"Well, honey, we're just kind of flipping around," my dad said.

My mom stretched and groaned. "There's never anything on. I don't know why we bother."

"That's not true," I said. "There's tons of great TV on all the time." I grabbed the remote from my dad and changed the channel to one of my favorite shows, *Daughter of the Devil*, about a high school girl whose dad is actually Satan. Unfortunately, right when I turned it on, the dad was in the middle of turning red and growing two horns.

"What is this?" my dad said, and not in a good way.

"It's not always this weird," I said quickly.

My mom put the television on mute. "Can I ask why you're hanging out with us, instead of in your usual spot at the opposite end of the house?"

I sighed. I wasn't really crazy about the idea of telling my parents what I was up to, because I knew they'd ask me a million questions. But I decided what the heck. It was easier just to come out with it.

"Ten friends and I decided to give up our phones for a week. And me personally, I'm giving up my computer, too."

My parents stared at me as if I'd just told them *I* was the Devil.

"Give up your phone, as in completely and totally not use it at all?" asked my mom.

I nodded.

My dad rubbed his eyes, as if he couldn't believe it was his daughter sitting in front of him. "I don't get it. How will you live? Isn't your phone kind of like oxygen? Isn't it possible you will actually suffocate without it?"

"Ha-ha," I answered.

"Well, I think it's wonderful," said my mom. "Good for you. Is this all because of your meeting with that singer?"

I stared at her. "That singer? *That singer?!*"

"Sorry," said my mom. "I forget her name right now."

"Jane," I said shortly. "Jane Plantero. She's a genius, so you should probably know her name."

"Got it," my dad said. "Jen Romero."

"Dad, you are just so hilarious tonight."

He grinned. "Thanks."

"And yes," I said, "meeting Jane did change my life, and this is part of that change."

My mom hugged me, and my dad leaned over and gave me a quick kiss on the cheek. "Well, we can thank whatever her name is," he said, "because I think it's pretty cool. And if it means we get to hang with you a bit more, well then, I'm all for that, too."

"Cool," I said. "Can I see the remote?"

"Of course, honey," said my mom, handing it to me.

I turned the sound back on just in time to see the dad eating his dinner with a pitchfork.

My dad rolled his eyes. "Seriously?"

"Yes, seriously," I said.

He harrumphed. "Fine, but only because this is a special occasion."

By the end of the episode, both my parents were hooked.

THE NEXT LETTER

Dear Jane,

I hope you're doing great!

I was so honored to meet you the other day, and was so inspired by your words. In fact, I wanted you to know that it's happening! I found ten friends, and together we've all decided to give up our cell phones for a whole week. We started today and will go all the way to our school talent show, which is this Saturday. Technically that's only six days, but I hope that's okay. We want to make a big announcement at the talent show and show everybody that we did it!

I am also working on the song and will send it to you as soon as it's done.

Thank you for trusting me. I promise to stick to my end of the bargain! I won't let you down.

Your absolutely biggest fan ever,

Katie Friedman

WRITING A SONG IS HARD, BUT MAKING A PHONE CALL IS HARDER

After _Daughter Of The Devil_, and after ice cream, and after playing with the dog, and after trying to play charades but realizing it's hard with three people, and after playing War instead, and after finishing my homework, and after writing a letter to Jane, and after doing everything possible that doesn't involve a cell phone and a computer, I got out my guitar and tried to write music for my song, "How."

It turns out writing music for a song is really, really hard.

It doesn't seem like it should be that hard to put a melody to a few words.

How do you
Speak the words
That you never thought would be spoken?

How do you
Break the heart
That never has been broken?

Pretty soon, I'd written a new verse:

How do you write a song
If you've never written one before?
How do you write a melody
That doesn't sound like nails on a chalkboard?

After about twenty minutes, I threw my guitar on my bed in disgust and reached for my phone to text Becca.

Except my phone wasn't there.

Ack!

Okay, fine. I'd call her.

Except my phone wasn't there.

Ack again!

I raced down the stairs.

"Mom? I need help!"

My mom was in the kitchen, making chicken soup from the leftover chicken. It smelled amazing.

"What's up?"

"I need to talk to Becca, but I don't have my phone, and she doesn't have her phone."

She stirred her soup. "Well, okay, so use our home phone. Do you know her number?"

"Of course I don't know her number! I don't even know how to FIND her number!"

My mom smiled. "Well, there are these things called phone books. You can use that."

"Where is it?"

"Good question." She rifled through a few drawers, looked in a few cabinets, then finally pulled out a tattered old book that looked like it was found in a Dumpster somewhere. "Here ya go!"

I picked it up. It was heavy. Who were all these people? I started thumbing through the pages—the print was tiny! After about two minutes, I finally found it: Clausen, 79 Sniffen Road (203) 555-0157.

Now all I had to do was find our phone.

I hadn't used it in about two years. Except for when Jane called me a few days before. Yeah, there was *that*.

I went to the place where it was supposed to be, and the receiver part was still there, but no phone.

"Has anyone seen the phone?"

They shrugged.

"Don't you guys know where it is?"

"It's probably where the remote is," said my dad. "I can never find that, either."

Great. I started overturning every cushion in the house, until I finally found it wedged underneath a couch in the living room.

"There you are," I muttered.

I dialed the number.

Nothing happened.

"Mom? Dad? The phone's not working!"

"Maybe it's out of battery."

"Try charging it."

I stared at the phone. I realized I was breathing hard. I was actually out of breath, just from trying to make a phone call.

Wow, I thought. *That's sad.*

I dropped the phone in my mom's lap.

"I'm going to bed," I said.

My dad chuckled.

"Welcome to 1987," he said.

29

THIRD LIE

The next day was Tuesday, the second day of our phone strike. Nothing that fascinating happened at school, except that Mr. Radonski, our crazy gym teacher, told me he was so inspired by what we were doing that he was going to give up his cell phone for a whole year.

"But Mr. Radonski," I reminded him, "then you won't be able to check the sports scores all during softball practice."

Mr. Radonski frowned. "Good point. Forget it," he said.

After school, I had a stop to make.

When my mom pulled into Nareem's driveway, I didn't get out of the car right away. She put the car in park and turned to me.

"What is it, honey?"

I stared straight ahead. "Well, he doesn't know I'm coming, since I didn't have my phone to call him, so I'm thinking maybe he's not home."

"Well, the only way to find out is if you get out of the car and ring the doorbell."

I sat there for another minute, doing neither of those things.

My mom turned the car all the way off. "Well?"

"I guess I'm a little nervous."

She rubbed the back of my shoulder. "This is worth talking about for a second. Do you know why you're nervous?"

I rolled my eyes. "Of course. Because I'm about to ask the boy whose feelings I hurt for another favor."

My mom shook her head. "Not exactly. You're nervous because you're about to ask the boy whose feelings you hurt for another favor *in person*. Ordinarily, you would have texted him. You would have texted, HEY I WROTE ANOTHER LETTER TO JANE, IF I LEAVE IT IN YOUR MAILBOX CAN YOUR DAD GIVE IT TO HER? And he would have texted you back, OKAY. But this way, you're forced to actually look him in the eye and ask him face-to-face. This is a good thing. This is what real communication is."

I stared straight ahead, out the windshield of the car and up toward Nareem's front door. It didn't really feel like a good thing. But I realized my mom was right.

"Okay, here goes."

My mom gave me a kiss for luck. "I'll be waiting right here."

I jumped out of the car and ran up to Nareem's front

door, almost as if I were worried that if I didn't do it quickly, I would change my mind. I rang the doorbell, and five seconds later the door opened.

Just like last time, it was Ru, Nareem's little sister. She looked up at me, but said nothing.

"Hi, Ru!" I said, a little too cheerfully. "Is your brother home?"

"Yes," she said, as if that was all I wanted to know.

"Well, could you please tell him I'm here?"

She thought that one over for a minute—long enough for me to actually wonder if Nareem had told her what happened—until she suddenly turned around and sprinted up the stairs.

I waited.

After pretty much the longest minute of my life, Nareem appeared at the door.

"Hi, Katie."

Way-too-bright smile. "Hi!"

We stared at each other for a minute.

"I thought I said we shouldn't talk for a while," he said, finally.

"I know. Can I come in anyway?"

Nareem stood off to the side of the door, a silent invitation to enter. I slipped past him and looked around his house like I'd never seen it before, even though I'd been there at least five times. Finally I forced myself to look at him.

"I have a favor to ask you. Just one thing, and then I promise, I won't bother you anymore."

He gave me a blank look. "What is it?"

I pulled the letter out of my bag. "I wrote another letter to Jane, to tell her the latest news."

"What latest news?"

"You know," I said. "That a whole bunch of us are giving up our cell phones for a week."

Nareem frowned. "Why would you need to tell her that?"

I realized that Nareem didn't know why this was so important to me. He didn't know about the deal I had with Jane.

"I just think she would really enjoy knowing that not only did I decide to give up my phone, ten other kids did, too," I told him. It was the third lie I'd told Nareem in three days. Who says face-to-face communication helps people connect? So far it just seemed like it was helping me become a better liar.

"Fine, yes. I will do it." Nareem held out his hand, and I gave him the letter.

Poor Nareem. He's such a good person that even when he wants to be mean, he can't pull it off. "Thank you so much, Nareem, you're the best. I'll see you tomorrow." I turned to head toward the door, but Nareem stopped me.

"If you don't mind, now I would like you to do something for me. Okay?"

I smiled. "Of course! Anything!" I breathed a huge sigh of relief. Nareem still cared about me enough to think I could do something to help him. I felt the warmth of relief spread through my body.

He pointed up the stairs. "All you have to do is come with me. I want to show you something."

I could hear his mom singing as we passed the kitchen. She was making something that smelled amazing. Every time I came to their house, Nareem's mother was making some incredible dish. It made me wish a little bit that my mom didn't have such a busy job, so she could stay home and cook more. But then I felt a little bad thinking that, and made myself stop.

We climbed the stairs and went into his room. He stopped. I stopped. I waited, but he didn't move.

"Nareem? What did you want to show me?"

He walked over to his desk and opened his computer. The screen-saver was a photograph.

Of me.

It was from the Plain Jane concert. My face was lit up with pure happiness as I watched the band onstage. My hands were in the air, and it looked as though I was dancing a little bit.

It was the first picture I'd ever seen of myself where I thought, hey, I actually *am* kind of pretty.

"When did you take that?"

"When you weren't looking."

"It's really nice."

"It is."

Nareem closed his eyes for a few seconds, then opened them again. Without another word he headed out of his room and back down the stairs. I followed.

He went to the front door and opened it. As I went through it, I stopped and looked at him.

"Why did you want to show me that picture?"

Nareem looked like he was trying to decide whether he wanted to speak or not. Finally he decided. "Jane was right about trying to connect with each other," he said. "She was right about trying to communicate. But sometimes memories are the only connection and the only communication we have."

I felt tears behind my eyes. "Thank you, Nareem," I said. "For everything. Thank you."

"You're welcome."

I didn't want him to see me cry, so I turned and headed to my mom's car.

"Katie."

I stopped and looked back. Nareem smiled sadly.

"I took that picture with my cell phone," he said.

MRS. KATZ

My mom asked me a bunch of questions on the way home, but I didn't feel like answering any of them. Eventually she left me alone, and let me put on Plain Jane. Since Nareem lived close to me, we only had time to listen to one song, and I picked "Houses"—an amazing song Jane wrote, about being a child of divorced parents.

> *Two warm beds*
> *Two kitchens*
> *Two places to be*
>
> *Two backyards*
> *Two front porches*
> *Two parents who don't agree*

A person who
Divides herself
Can never truly be free

So why do I
Have two houses
When there's only one me.

"Wow," said my mom. "Intense."

"That's one word for it," I said. "*Awesome* is another."

My mom looked thoughtful. "Maybe her parents weren't honest with her about what was going on, and that's why she's so focused on people communicating with one another."

There goes Mom, putting her therapist hat on again.

When we pulled into our driveway, there was a strange car there. It took me a minute to realize whose car it was.

Jake's mom's.

I mentioned her before, right? I think I did. I can't remember. Anyway, in case I didn't, here's a quick reminder: She's a little crazy.

Mrs. Katz is one of those moms who is in their kid's business all the time. I mean, *all the time*. She wants to know where Jake is, what he's doing, and why he's doing it, every second of every day. She's kind of out of control about it. I think they call them "helicopter parents" now, because of the way they hover over your every move. Anyway, she was one.

Which is why I was pretty sure I knew why she was at our house.

"There you are!" she shouted, when my mom and I walked through the door. Jake was there, too, looking embarrassed. And my dad, who was never a huge fan of Mrs. Katz's, looked incredibly relieved to see us.

"Mitzi," said my mom sweetly. "How nice to see you."

Katz   Cat

I'd forgotten her first name was Mitzi! What a great name! For a cat. Which I guess made sense, since she was a Katz.

"Claire, I'm not here on a social call," Mrs. Katz (Mitzi) said. "I'm here because our children have taken it upon themselves to do something completely unacceptable."

I sat down next to Jake. We glanced at each other and tried not to laugh. This was going to be good. I felt a big *plop!* on the other side and turned to see my dad had joined us on the couch. Apparently he was going to let my mom do the talking on this one.

"Are you referring to the kids giving up their cell phones?" asked my mom. "Because I have to say, I find it quite admirable."

Mrs. Katz snorted. "Admirable, perhaps, but not practical." She pulled out her own cell phone. "Can I tell you how many text messages I send to Jake on a given day?" She stared at her phone, counting. "Upwards of forty! He needs lunch, he needs to be picked up, he needs books, he needs his computer, he needs his cello, his baseball glove—"

"Actually, I don't really need my baseball glove," Jake interrupted, "since I only play about one inning per game." The three of us on the couch laughed, and even my mom stifled a giggle, but Mitzi wasn't amused.

"And last night!" she stammered. "When I couldn't reach Jake, I thought the worst. The worst! I had to call the school to find out what was going on. But what if, God forbid, something actually does happen to one of our children?" She shook her head. "I don't like this little experiment, I don't like it at all."

"Mitzi," my mom said, in her calmest, most soothing professional therapist voice, "I completely understand your concern. In fact, I share it, to some degree. But I think our kids are doing something brave. It's terrific that they've realized how addicted they've become to their phones, and that they've decided to do something about it. And as you and I both know, what they're addicted to is not the staying-in-touch-with-their-parents part. It's all the other stuff, the silly stuff, and the stuff that distracts them from living, and learning, and growing."

I stared up at my mom, amazed at how smart she was, and how she could say what she was thinking so perfectly. And what *I* was thinking, too, actually.

Mitzi sniffed the air, like she smelled something bad. "Yes, I understand all that. Truly I do. But it doesn't do me any good when I can't text my son to find out what time cello rehearsal will be done, or which court he's on for his tennis lesson."

I looked at Jake. "You take tennis?"

"Not by choice," he answered.

Finally my dad decided to enter the conversation. "Mrs. Katz, can I ask you something?"

"Absolutely," she said.

He stood up and took out his cell phone. "Did you have one of these when you were growing up?"

Mrs. Katz made a face. "Of course not."

"Neither did I," said my dad. "Can you believe it? No cell phone! No texting! And you know what else? No computer, no Internet, and no e-mail either!"

"What's your point, Jack?" Mrs. Katz whimpered.

"My point is, we survived," said my dad. "We did okay. In fact, we did better than okay!" He smiled, satisfied, and sat back down on the couch.

Jake's mom made a face at her son—*we need to run away from these strange people*, I think it said—and picked up her purse. "It's a different world now," she sniffed. "A faster world, a crazier world, a more competitive world. Everyone is on the go all the time. If you don't keep up, you fall behind. That's all I'm saying. Thank you for listening."

"Well, thanks for stopping by," said my mom, holding the door open.

Mrs. Katz saved her last comment for me. "Katie, I'm sorry to ruin your admirable little experiment, but Jake will be taking his phone back tomorrow."

On the way out the door, Jake caught my eye.

"No, I won't," he whispered.

A DAY IN THE LIFE OF
NO PHONES

The next day at lunch, I found myself sitting between Tiffany and Amber—the two Elizettes.

I can safely say that was the first time that had ever happened.

Except for the day before.

It had been only two days, but what was happening

was obvious. The people with no phones were starting to hang around together. And not only that, we were actually getting to know and like each another. At lunch, we made sure we all sat at one table.

"I think it's so awesome that you're in a band," Tiffany said to me. "I've always wanted to play a musical instrument."

"You don't really have to play an instrument to be in a band," said Becca, who was also sitting with us. "In fact, I barely do."

"That's not true," I said.

"Um, yeah, it is," Becca said.

Tiffany smiled a little sadly. "I don't have any talent. I'm still waiting to discover what I'm talented at, but so far I haven't figured it out."

"That's crazy," I said. Tiffany laughed, a little embarrassed. I couldn't believe it. Eliza, Tiffany, and Amber were on the very top rung of the middle school social ladder. They were as put-together and popular as it gets. It was amazing to hear that any one of them could be insecure about anything.

"Hey, let's play a game," Celia said. "Everyone say something about themselves that nobody else knows. I'll go first." She closed her eyes for a second then blurted out, "I want to have seven children. Four boys and three girls." Then she stared right at her boyfriend, Phil Manning. His eyes popped out of his head.

"Wow," said Phil.

"Awkward," said Ricky.

"I'll go next," said Amber. "Every night before I go to bed I pray that when I wake up my pillows will be made of marshmallows."

"Cool!" exclaimed Hannah. "Has it ever happened?"

"Not yet," admitted Amber.

"Oh, darn," said Hannah. "Call me when it does. I love marshmallows."

Amber smiled brightly. "I totally will!"

I should point out here that this was probably the longest conversation Amber and Hannah had ever had with each other.

Eliza raised her hand. "I have something," she said.

We all turned, waiting for her to continue.

"Sometimes I hate being super pretty."

Everyone stared at her, not sure if she was kidding or not.

"I know you guys think I'm being a big bragger or obnoxious or something," she said. "But I'm not. I'm being serious. I know I'm pretty. I can tell by the way everyone treats me and looks at me and how people want to hang around with me."

Amber and Tiffany looked at each other, then at the ground.

"And it is awesome a lot of the time," Eliza went on. "But not always. Sometimes it's weird and uncomfortable and

147

I know people make fun of me because they resent me and sometimes I wish I looked more like regular people." Suddenly she looked right at me. "Like Katie."

"Uh, that sounded like an insult," I said. "Just sayin'."

"I'm sorry! You know what I mean," said Eliza. "You're really cute. But you're not so pretty that it's the only thing people say or think about you. They think about how you're smart, and funny, and nice, too. With me, people only think one thing. Beauty. And yeah, it's a good thing, but I'm a lot more than that."

Eliza stopped talking and took a few deep breaths, like talking that much had exhausted her. And maybe it had. I'd never heard her say so many words in a row in my life.

"I think you're more than just pretty," Jackie offered. "I've always thought you had a great sense of style."

"Yeah," added Celia. "I love your clothes. A lot."

"Thanks, you guys," Eliza said, but she didn't seem all that cheered up.

"I don't think that's what she's talking about," Jake said. "Style, clothes—it's all part of the same thing. Eliza's saying she's tired of being judged by her appearance. She wants other kids to look beneath the surface."

"Yes!" Eliza said, staring at Jake as if seeing him for the first time. Which she was, in a way.

"I'll be honest with you," Becca said to Eliza. "I've never really liked looking beneath your surface. Because when

I did, I saw a girl who just loved being the prettiest and didn't mind letting other people know she loved being the prettiest."

Everyone froze.

"What?" Becca said, defensively. "Isn't this what this is all about? I bet everyone at this table has texted that very same thing about Eliza to somebody else. Because we've all thought it at some point or another. Well, guess what? Nobody has their phones now, and nobody has the chance to text behind anybody's back, so I'm just trying to get in the spirit of honesty and open communication and all that." She turned to Eliza. "I'm sorry. And you know what? The fact that you just said what you said makes me see you in a totally different way. I'm sorry I judged you."

We all looked at Eliza, wondering how she'd react. The first thing she did was flip her hair—an unconscious move that she did all the time.

"No, you're right," she said to Becca. "Usually I do love that people think I'm super pretty. And I guess I can be obnoxious about it sometimes."

"There's nothing wrong with being proud of who you are," Jake chimed in. "I love being the smartest, for example."

Hannah elbowed him in the ribs. "Who says you're the smartest?"

"You do," Jake told her.

Hannah shrugged. "I was just trying to make you feel good."

"Can we move on?" Ricky said. "Yay for Eliza and her feelings and all that, but we have a lot more people to get through if we're going to hear one secret from everyone."

Suddenly a huge burst of laughter came from down the row. We all looked up and saw Timmy, Charlie Joe, and Pete staring at one of their phones and cracking up.

"Must be the latest video of a cat riding a pig," Jackie said.

"Yeah, give me a break," Phil said. He stood up. "What are you guys watching? Let me guess—there's poop involved."

Everyone at our table cracked up, including me.

Charlie Joe looked up. Then he elbowed Pete and Timmy and they looked up, too.

"Are you guys getting in touch with your feelings?" Charlie Joe yelled over at us.

"Yeah, *are* you?" Pete echoed, not very imaginatively.

I stood up. "We're just having a normal conversation, Charlie Joe," I said.

"It's called 'communicating without being snarky or mean,'" Hannah added. "You should try it some time."

Charlie Joe turned red. He'd had a massive crush on Hannah pretty much forever, and the fact that she had just talked snarkily to him was devastating. Or, it would have been devastating, if it had been anyone other than Charlie Joe Jackson.

"I get it," he said, making a quick recovery. "You guys think you're superior, because you're not using your phones for a whole week. Well, whoop-dee-doo for you."

"Yeah, whoop-dee-do," Timmy said, who apparently was just as original as Pete.

"That's not true. We don't think we're better than anyone," I said, but I wasn't sure I believed myself. Charlie Joe was right: It had only been a couple of days, but those of us without phones were starting to form a little club, and people who still had their phones weren't really invited.

"You're too good to sit with us," Timmy said. "We get it."

"Timmy," Phil said, then stopped. Phil did that a lot—said the first word of a sentence, then stopped. If anyone else did it, kids would get annoyed, but since Phil looked more like a high school football player than any other kid in middle school, we all just learned to patiently wait for him to say whatever it was he was going to say next.

"Yeah?" Timmy said, eventually.

Phil thought for another minute. "The point is that you're here talking to us about this face-to-face," he said. "Ordinarily you would be texting us these insults. This is a big improvement. I'm glad you are enough of a man to talk honestly."

Pete elbowed Timmy, "Hey, you're a man!"

"Cool," Timmy answered.

"Congratulations," said Becca.

It seemed like everyone was going to be friends with each other again, but then Charlie Joe got out his phone and punched a few keys.

"Hey, look!" he exclaimed. "Plain Jane just announced their new contest!"

Timmy and Pete immediately checked their own phones.

"Huh?" Timmy said.

Charlie Joe showed them his phone. "Free tickets to their next concert for anyone named Katie Friedman! Text I LOVE CELL PHONES to claim your prize!"

They all starting convulsing with laughter.

"Ha-ha-ha," I said, scowling at him.

"Charlie Joe, stop being so annoying," Eliza said. "Please

take your phony phone-using self back to your phony phone-using table."

That cracked Ricky up. "Yeah, phonies!" he said. "Go phone somewhere else!"

Everyone laughed and repeated the word *phonies*. All of a sudden we had a new nickname for the phone-users of the world.

"If we're phonies," Charlie Joe said, "then you're cavemen. You're living in prehistoric times."

"Yeah, you're cavemen," Pete said. "You should probably leave now so you can start hunting for dinner." Then he laughed way too loudly at his own joke.

"Okay, enough you guys," I said. "Charlie Joe, let's not turn this into a big thing. You're obviously entitled to your phones and your texting and whatever, just like we're entitled to sit at lunch and have interesting conversations."

Charlie Joe raised an eyebrow. "So you're saying people with phones don't have interesting conversations?"

I sighed. "I'm saying when everyone is staring down at the little device in their hands, there's not a lot of connecting going on. Like right now. We're disagreeing, we're getting on each other's nerves, but at least we're connecting. Right? That's what this week is all about." I paused, because I wasn't sure I should say what I was about to say. But then I said it anyway. "If it's too intense for you, that's fine. You can go back to your cat videos and Instagrams and Snapchats. What we're doing isn't for everyone. I get it."

Charlie Joe stopped smiling at that moment, and looked at me for a minute like he didn't know who I was. "Wow, Katie. I never thought I'd see the day when you would actually say out loud that you thought you were better than me."

"I'm not saying I'm better than you," I said. "Different, that's all."

Charlie Joe shook his head slowly. The fun and games were over.

"Let's go, you guys," he said. "The cavemen are too good for us. Let's go back to the twenty-first century where we belong."

"Yeah," Timmy said.

"Let's," Pete said.

As we watched them walk away, Ricky muttered, "See ya later, phonies."

"Phonies!" Tiffany squealed, laughing. "What a hilarious nickname."

As everyone got busy congratulating one another for being so clever, I kept watching Charlie Joe. He was staring down at his phone, but I'm not sure he was reading anything. I felt bad. I felt good. I felt guilty. I felt proud. I felt happy. I felt sad. And I felt right.

Communicating is complicated.

IT'S FOR YOU

So it was official: There was an "us versus them" thing going on.

The war escalated in language arts, when Ms. Kransky asked me and Jake to talk in front of the class about our decision to give up our phones.

"I would like everyone to hear from these impressive young students, who have recognized a problem and are trying to do something about it," she said. "We can all learn something from them."

Talk about a foolproof way to get everyone to hate you.

Two minutes after we started talking about how great it was to sit at lunch and actually look at each other, among other wonderful things about a phone-free existence, an actual phone started ringing.

Charlie Joe held his hand up.

"I think I'm getting a call," he said. He got out his phone. "Hello?" Charlie Joe listened for a second. Then he held the phone out toward me. "It's for Katie."

"Charlie Joe, put that away," Ms. Kransky ordered.

Charlie Joe looked concerned. "What if it's an emergency?"

For a second I got scared. Could he possibly not be making a joke for once?

"CHARLIE JOE!" commanded Ms. Kransky.

"Okay, fine," Charlie Joe said, putting away his phone. "But you get my point. If someone really did have something important to tell Katie, or Jake, or any one of the Cavemen who gave up their phones, how would they do it? What if it was an emergency? Cell phones are not horrible. They're incredibly useful. They can even help save lives."

"You're making a good point," Ms. Kransky said. "You're just making it the wrong way. One more stunt like that and you'll be in detention."

"Yes, Ms. Kransky," Charlie Joe said sweetly.

Then, incredibly, another phone beeped.

Nareem's, of all people.

He turned red and fumbled for his phone.

Ms. Kranksy had had enough. "TURN ALL PHONES OFF!"

"Sorry," Nareem mumbled. "My mother sometimes texts to ask me what I'd like for dinner.

"And THAT sums up the problem," Ms. Kransky said. "Charlie Joe is right, phones and texting can be wonderful tools. But that's lost under all the unnecessary noise and distractions and time wasting they also cause."

Jake and I nodded solemnly in agreement.

"Thank you, kids," Ms. Kransky said to us. "You may return to your seats."

We sat down.

"And I'm sure Charlie Joe apologizes for calling you 'Cavemen,'" Ms. Kransky added, shaking her head.

"Oh, we don't mind," Jake said. "We kind of like it, actually."

I smiled, adding, "It's better than being called 'Phonies.'"

SHOW ME YOUR MOVES

I've always loved recess—who doesn't?—so I'm really happy we still have it in middle school. The adults say it "helps the students exercise their bodies and exercise their social skills."

I don't know about that, but it's definitely nice to get outside in the middle of the day.

You can do whatever you want at recess. Some kids play sports, other kids gossip, a few kids read quietly. It's usually pretty much a free-for-all, with the boys going one way and the girls going another.

But that doesn't mean the boys don't text the girls the entire time. And vice versa.

But that week, things were different.

After a few days, us Cavemen had our recess routine down: head to the far end of the blacktop to hang out. Monday, Celia and Jackie had discovered that they each

liked knitting, so they started bringing their stuff to school
and knitting matching sweaters for their two favorite teachers to give as end-of-year presents. And on Tuesday, Eliza
and I realized that her birthday was the same as my mom's,
and they both loved roller coasters, so we decided to have
a big double-birthday bash at Six Flags. (It won't ever
happen—trust me—but it sounded awesome at the time.)

By Wednesday's recess, one thing was clear: the Phonies were pretty tired of watching the Cavemen become
one big happy family, and they were ready to do something about it.

I first noticed something was different when I got outside and Pete was hanging out on our side of the blacktop
with his obnoxious friend Eric, who I hadn't liked ever
since fourth grade, when I saw him pick his nose and wipe
it on the shirt of the girl in front of him (she never noticed,
luckily).

The rest of the Cavemen were hanging back, not sure
what to do.

I went up to Pete. "What are you guys up to?"

Pete shrugged. "What do you mean, what are we up to?"

"I don't know," I said. "I just thought, you know, like
this is usually where *we* hang out."

He smirked. "It's a free country, last I checked."

Then Eric got out his cell phone and punched in a number. "We're ready," he said into the phone.

Suddenly it seemed like the whole grade was running

over to the blacktop. They were all holding something over their heads. As they got closer, I could tell what they were.

Cell phones.

Timmy and Charlie Joe were in front of everyone else, as they came running up to me and the rest of the Cavemen.

"Everybody ready?" Timmy yelled.

"Yeah!" everybody answered.

Charlie Joe cupped his hands to his mouth. "1 . . . 2 . . . 3!"

On "3," everyone pushed a button, and a song began to play. On everyone's phones. At the exact same time. Loudly.

"Show Me Your Moves," by Plain Jane.

Definitely her dance-iest song.

> *Show me your moves*
> *And I'll show you mine*
> *We can decide*
> *Whose moves are more fine*
>
> *Show me some style*
> *Show me finesse*
> *And I'll show you how good*
> *I can look in this dress.*
>
> *Show me the right stuff*
> *And leave out the wrong*
> *And I'll show you I love you*
> *'Til the end of the song.*

Suddenly, the blacktop was covered with people. And they were all dancing. People who think dancing is the dorkiest thing in the world were dancing. People who think dancing at recess is even dorkier were dancing. Even Charlie Joe Jackson was dancing.

Everyone was dancing.

And it turns out fifty cell phones playing the same song can make a pretty loud racket.

Charlie Joe came over to me and smiled. I tried to smile back.

"I thought you were way too cool to ever dance!" I shouted. "Especially at recess!"

"It's a special occasion!" he shouted back. "This is my favorite Plain Jane song! It doesn't have one of her preachy messages. It's just plain fun!" And he danced away.

Meanwhile, the only people not dancing were the Cavemen. We watched, not sure what to do. We all looked at each other.

I walked over to Becca. "Can you believe this?"

She shook her head. At least, I thought she shook her head. But then it kept shaking, and I realized that she was actually moving to the beat.

"Becca!" I said.

She looked at me. "What? I love this song!" And in the next instant, she ran out to the blacktop and joined the dance party.

The rest of the Cavemen followed in two seconds.

I was the last one standing on the sidelines. Even Eliza, my cofounder of the Cavemen, was out there, dancing up a storm. "Sorry," she mouthed to me, while slithering up to Charlie Joe.

I watched, wanting desperately to join in, but I couldn't.

I was either too proud or too annoyed. Probably both. After a few seconds, I felt someone come up beside me. It was Ms. Ferrell, my guidance counselor.

"You guys should play this at the talent show," she said.

34

WHAT THE HEART WANTS

That night we hit the halfway point—which meant the Halfway Point Barbecue.

I was getting ready to go to Tiffany's house when my mom knocked on my door.

"You have a phone call."

I could tell who it was by the amazed smile on her face.

I raced to the kitchen to pick up the phone. "Hello?"

"Well, hey there," came that familiar, rock 'n' roll voice. "Just checkin' in. Glad to hear you're holding up your end of the bargain."

"You got my note?" I stammered.

"Yes, ma'am!"

My heart was racing in the usual I-can't-believe-I'm-talking-to-Jane-Plantero way. "I was really hoping to talk to you again. We're halfway through the week."

"And how's it going?"

"Well, it's been pretty interesting so far."

Jane let out a raspy chuckle. "I'll bet. Yup, Nareem's Papa gave me the note. How are things with ole Nareem, anyway?"

I took a deep breath. "Well, I should probably tell you—Nareem and I broke up. After the whole text thing. He's such an incredible person, though."

"Well," Jane said, "the heart wants what it wants."

I nodded, even though she couldn't see me. "The funny thing is, there's this other boy, who I have kind of a complicated relationship with. And he didn't give up his cellphone for the week. And in fact, it's become this thing at school, the kids who gave up their phones against the kids who didn't. And he's leading the other side. And it's really annoying."

Jane laughed again, harder this time, and it ended with a coughing fit.

"Are you all right?" I asked.

"I'm fine," she said, still chuckling and coughing a bit. "You join the rock 'n' roll club, you sign up for a lot of late nights. It's in the manual. Nothin' I can do about it."

"Okay," I said. I wanted to tell her to take care of herself, but didn't want to sound like a priss.

"Enough about me," she answered. "Sounds like you've got a lot on your plate. And how about the song? 'Bout done with that baby yet?"

"I'm working on it," I said, somewhat untruthfully.

"Well, work harder," Jane said. "Don't you have a talent show coming up?"

"Saturday night. We have rehearsal Friday. I'll finish it by then, I promise."

"Good girl." I heard some muffled sounds—I think someone was saying something to Jane, and Jane answered—then she said to me, "Gotta fly. You take care. You're doing good." And then there was a click.

I hung up the phone, thinking about what Jane said. *The heart wants what it wants.*

Well, right at that moment, my heart was thinking about CHICKMATE. And my heart didn't care that Becca and the rest of the girls in the band just wanted to play famous songs.

Some day, I was going to play *my* song.

THE HIGH POINT

Tiffany lived in one of those houses that's way bigger than it needs to be. Does anyone really need a fifth bathroom? Or a third car in the garage? Or a first sitting room? I don't even know what a sitting room is. All I know is, no one ever sits in them.

But Tiffany's extra-huge house also meant that it was an amazing place for a barbecue. She had a pool, a tennis court, and even a croquet course that her dad set up.

Unfortunately, the Cavemen weren't using any of those things.

Instead, we were sitting on the (giant) porch, playing another game. This time, we each had to confess about a text we'd sent about someone in the group, behind their back.

The game was Tiffany's idea, so she went first. "I once sent a text about Celia," she said. "It was when you started going out with Phil. I sent a text to Eliza that I thought he was just going out with you to make Eliza jealous."

"Huh?" Phil said. "That's not true!"

"I remember that," Eliza confirmed.

Celia looked surprised, but also a little proud.

"I'm really sorry," Tiffany said. "It was really immature of me. You two are like the most awesome couple."

"It's okay," Celia told Tiffany. "I once sent a text to Jill Kerhsaw, saying that I thought your highlights looked fake."

Tiffany's jaw dropped. "Seriously?"

Celia nodded and giggled.

"Uh-oh," Hannah said. "Tiffany takes her hair very seriously."

"I do not!" Tiffany said. "Well, maybe a little," she added, giggling.

Eliza was the only one who didn't laugh at that. Looking very serious, she said, "I'll go next." Then she turned to me. "Katie, I remember texting Amber and Tiffany that you could be really mean."

To say I was caught off guard would be an understatement. "Huh?" I managed to stammer.

Hannah tried to rescue me. "Does anyone want to play pool volleyball?"

But nobody moved.

"We're being honest, right?" Eliza said. "No hiding behind phones or texts?"

I nodded. "Yeah."

"Well," Eliza continued, "I think you always knew I liked Charlie Joe, and I think you thought it was funny that he didn't like me back, because he liked Hannah. And I heard that you made fun of me on text a lot, like about my asking you for help on homework and stuff, which really hurt my feelings and made me feel stupid. So I was wondering if it was true—if you ever sent mean texts to anyone about me."

WOW.

There it was.

The most honest thing any of us had ever said to anyone else.

I turned red. Everyone waited to see if I would be honest back.

"I did," I said finally. "I sent mean texts about you wanting my help with homework and not knowing the answer to something in class and stuff like that. But I never thought you were stupid, just lazy. Like you could get away with not working hard because you're pretty. And you're right. I did think it was funny that you liked goofy Charlie Joe Jackson, and he didn't like you back. I never thought about your feelings being hurt. I'm really sorry."

DOUBLE WOW.

The porch was silent. The only sound you could hear was the sprinkler on the clay tennis court, whirring around, spraying water.

"It's okay," Eliza said to me, finally. "I understand." And we hugged.

"Wow, that was intense, you guys," Ricky said.

"I can honestly say that wouldn't have happened if we had our phones," Jake added.

Everyone else agreed.

"Burgers are ready!" yelled some adult.

We ate, and then we decided what the heck, we'd play some croquet after all. While whacking the ball around the lawn, I felt really tired, but happy. This was what Jane meant by communication and connection. The next two days were going to be even better, and then I could tell Jane we did it! Backstage tour, here we come!

And then came Thursday morning.

MISSING

I'd just gotten off the bus and was on my way to homeroom when Hannah came running up to me.

"Katie! Come quick!"

"What? What happened?"

She didn't answer. But I could tell by her face that it wasn't good.

I followed her around the corner and down the hall, trying to figure out where she was going. Finally she began to slow down, and I realized we were by the lockers.

My locker.

Just to remind you, I basically never go to my locker in school. I don't even *lock* my locker. Most kids don't. The lockers are too far away from the classrooms, and kids are far too lazy to drop stuff off there in between classes. We'd rather lug our entire lives around in our backpacks.

So I hadn't been to my locker in four days—the last time was when I put everyone's phones there.

Which is why when I saw the door swinging open and the bag of phones sticking out, a sick feeling came over me.

The feeling that said, *I should have locked my locker*.

I walked past a few kids who were standing around, grabbed the bag, looked inside, and breathed an immediate sigh of relief. The phones were still there!

I quickly scanned the rest of my locker. "I don't think anything's missing," I said. "But then why would someone go into my locker?"

Hannah shook her head. "This is middle school that's why."

I started to put the bag back, but Hannah put her hand on my arm. "Hold on. Maybe you should count them."

"Count them?"

"Yup," Hannah said. "I'm sure they're all there, but just to be sure."

Another uneasy feeling came over me as I realized she was right. Just because someone hadn't stolen the bag didn't mean someone hadn't stolen *something*.

I counted.

Ten phones.

I counted again.

Ten phones again.

"One's missing," I said, my voice barely audible.

Hannah's eyes went wide. "Are you sure?"

I counted again. "Yup, I'm sure. There are supposed to be eleven phones here. There are only ten." I couldn't believe it, but I had to say it.

"Someone took a phone."

Then I thought something almost funny. I thought, *I should text Eliza and tell her what's going on.*

I think that's what they call "irony."

Hannah grabbed the bag from me and we counted the phones again. Then we turned every phone on to see whose they were, and we were able to figure out that it was Jake's phone that was missing.

"I can't believe it!" Hannah said. "Who would do this?"

"Who do you think?" By the look on Hannah's face I could tell she was thinking the same thing. Or should I say, the same person.

Charlie Joe.

WHO DID IT?

At lunch, we all tried to make Jake feel better about his stolen phone. He was really quiet though, and didn't feel much like talking.

Meanwhile, we still hadn't solved the mystery, so things were getting tense.

When I asked Charlie Joe if he'd taken it, he was offended. "You're crazy," he said. "I would never do something that predictable. Give me a little credit."

When I thought about it, he was right. His schemes usually had a lot more imagination to them.

My attention turned to Pete Milano, but it turned out he wasn't in school that day. He was "sick," which, amazingly enough, seemed to happen whenever there was a test he didn't want to take.

As usual, the Cavemen were all sitting together. Also as

usual, the Phonies were one table over. They were yakking and texting about the phone theft.

"Phone-tastic news!" Timmy hollered.

"I've never had so much phone in my life!" crowed his annoying friend Eric.

"E.T. phone home?" asked Charlie Joe. Then he launched into a bad E.T. voice. "I would, but I can't find it!"

The whole cafeteria laughed, except our table. We sat there, glumly.

Finally Ricky smacked his hand on his tray, spilling some of his chocolate milk. "Enough! I'm sick of this. I want my phone back. I'm sick of being a Caveman. I want to be back with everyone else."

"Me, too," said Phil. Which meant Celia did, too, since they agreed on everything.

Amber eyed me suspiciously. "Katie, how do we know you didn't take your own phone back, too? Everyone knows you like Charlie Joe. Maybe you wanted to do some text flirting."

Eliza looked at me with shocked eyes. "Wait a second, *you* like Charlie Joe?"

"Where have you been?" Jackie mumbled, giggling.

I felt my skin start to burn. "Me, like Charlie Joe? Ha! That's hilarious coming from you, Amber. You're just trying to protect Eliza, since you've worshipped the ground she's walked on for like five years."

Amber's face turned the color of tomato juice. "I have *not*!"

"You *have*, *too*!"

"ENOUGH!" Hannah yelled, slamming her own hand on the table.

I suddenly felt ashamed. "I'm sorry," I said to Amber. "This is stupid. We can't start fighting now. We're too close to the end of the week! Let's just be proud of what we're doing, and finish the week out strong."

Ricky rolled his eyes. "Finish the week out strong," he muttered. "Whatever."

"Yeah, whatever, " Tiffany said. "It's not so great not having a phone, Katie. Sorry, but it's true. I know we've had some good conversations and everything but otherwise it's really kind of boring."

A few heads nodded. I started to get nervous. I could probably convince Jane that one dropout was okay. But the whole thing looked like it was about to blow up.

"Only a few more days, you guys," I said. "Then, at the talent show, we can celebrate. And just wait—soon after that, we're going to celebrate again, and it's going to be amazing, trust me. We just have to finish out the week. Trust me, it's going to be awesome."

"What do you mean by that?" asked Ricky.

"Yeah, *what's* going to be awesome?" echoed Jake.

Everybody looked at me. I wasn't sure what to say.

Obviously I couldn't tell them about my deal with Jane, but I couldn't pretend I hadn't said it, either.

I tried to come up with something. "Um, I just meant that maybe we'll get some kind of award from the school or something."

"Whoop-de-doo," Ricky said. "We've given up our phones for a week and nobody even cares. The rest of the school thinks we're dorks, and you know what? They're right. We *are* dorks."

"That's crazy," Hannah said. "We're doing something cool, something no one's ever done before."

Becca cleared her throat. She's a pretty quiet person, plus she's like eleven feet tall, so when she talks, people listen. Everybody waited, curious to hear what she had to say.

"I kind of agree with Ricky," she said. "I'm not really sure what this whole thing is about, to be honest. I never considered myself addicted to my phone. And yeah, some kids definitely use their phones too much, but this seems extreme. It's just not how the world works these days. Charlie Joe is right. What if there's a real emergency and someone is trying to reach you? You need a phone. Everyone has one. If you don't have a phone you're literally missing the world going by."

Then Becca looked right at me. "Not everybody cares about things as much as you do, Katie, and it makes you kind of bossy sometimes."

I felt the sting of tears behind my eyes, but luckily, that's where they stayed.

Becca sat back down. Nobody moved for a second, then people started nodding. The tide was turning, and she was the one who turned it.

Suddenly I didn't have the energy to fight it anymore. We weren't going to make it. Jane would never hear my song, and why? Because of the co-leader of my band, that's why.

"Fine," I said. "Whoever wants to drop out, go ahead. All I know is, we wouldn't be having this kind of conversation *right now* if we had our phones. Becca, you'd be texting what you just said about me to Ricky. And Ricky would forward it to Tiffany and everyone would think it was hilarious, except for me, because I wouldn't be in on it. Cell phones cause secrets, and secrets cause lies—and lies hurt people."

"I like to think I can tell you anything," Becca said to me.

I fake smiled. "Well, you can definitely insult me to my face, that's for sure."

Becca looked wounded. "I wasn't trying to insult you. I was just trying to be honest. Didn't you just say that's what this was all about?"

"Well, thanks for the honesty," I said. "Let's just forget it. Whoever wants their cell phone back, just come meet me at my locker after lunch."

"Yeah, if you don't want us, we don't want you," Eliza added. "We started this by ourselves, and we can finish it together."

I wasn't sure that made sense, but I knew what she was getting at.

I waited for someone to come to my rescue, but nobody did.

"Okay," I said at last. It was really over.

Then, as I got up to put my tray away, I heard a familiar *DING DONG*.

A sound that hadn't been heard at our lunch table all week.

The sound of an incoming text.

Everybody froze in their seats. Waiting. Because the sound always came a second time.

And sure enough, five seconds later: *DING DONG!*

Even Charlie Joe could hear it at the next table. "What was that?" he said. "Was that what I think it was?"

Suddenly Phil shot to his feet. "Give it up!" he said. "Whoever has Jake's phone, give it up! Take the phone out and fess up!"

We sat still as statues, staring at each other.

Finally, the last person I would suspect reached into his pocket and placed his cell phone on the table.

Jake himself.

I stared in disbelief. "Wait a second. Your phone wasn't stolen? You . . . *took it yourself?*"

He nodded, head down in shame.

Jake Katz. One of the most well-behaved, agreeable kids in school, the one who always played by the rules, the one who never did anything to make anyone upset. The one kid you could count on.

We all stared at him.

"I'm sorry," he mumbled, so softly you could barely hear him. "I'm so sorry. It's just . . . I didn't know what to do . . . my mom was so mad. I'm . . ." He stopped for a second to check the text he got, then sent a quick reply. "Plus, I really missed playing Words with Friends. I was in the middle of a tournament." He sighed in defeat. "I guess I'm kind of addicted to that game."

Hannah looked shocked. "Why did you leave the locker open?" she asked.

"I wasn't going to," Jake said. "But somebody walked by and I—I guess I panicked."

I was too surprised to speak, at first. I thought about everything that had happened—Eliza telling me I was mean, Amber saying everyone knew I liked Charlie Joe, Becca calling me bossy, and now Jake betraying the whole group by taking his phone.

My heart sunk, and a weird burning sensation started pounding inside my head.

I trust you, Jane had said. If I deserved that trust, I'd have to tell her what happened. I'd have to tell her that I hadn't quite lived up to my end of the deal.

Which would mean no backstage tour for all of us at a concert.

And no Plain Jane playing my song.

"THAT'S HORRIBLE!" I yelled suddenly, before I could stop myself. "You stink! We had a deal! We were all in this together! I hate you! You ruined everything!"

Jake froze in shock. Everyone stared at me like I was an alien creature.

"Plus you could be suspended for going into my locker," I added for good measure.

Hannah looked furious. "What is *wrong* with you, Katie?! It's just a cell phone. It's not the end of the world."

I felt tears spring to my eyes. "You don't understand . . .

I had everything planned . . . it had to be ten people. It was going to be a surprise . . ."

"What was?" Hannah asked.

"OH, FORGET IT!" I yelled, and stared down at my plate.

Before anyone else could react, Eliza reached across the table and put her hand on Jake's arm. "Well, you know what? I'm actually not mad at you, Jake. It's okay. There were about a thousand times when I wanted to go into Katie's locker and get my phone. We get it." Eliza looked around the table. "Right, you guys?"

No one was sure what to do or say, so everyone just sat there for a few seconds.

"Yeah," Becca said, finally. "We were just about to bag this whole thing and get our phones anyway. Don't worry about it."

Jake finally picked his head up. "Seriously? You guys aren't mad?"

More kids started nodding. "Dude, my parents have been driving me crazy," Ricky said. "They used to tell me to put my phone away, but now they're all like, 'When are you getting your phone back? We need to be able to reach you!'"

"I have to admit," Jake said, "it's been kind of nice without my mom texting me every five minutes. I'm going to miss that."

Everyone laughed, except me. The nicer everyone was being, the more I felt like a jerk.

Hannah looked around, shaking her head. "You guys are amazing. You're being so nice to Jake. You're like the best friends anyone could have." Then she stood up. "And you know what? This is like a sign. We're in this together. We're Cavemen! And we're going to finish out the week as Cavemen!"

"Yeah!" Ricky said. "Cavemen all the way!"

Everyone around the table started high-fiving each other and chanting: "Cavemen! Cavemen! Cavemen!"

Mid-chant, Phil pointed at Charlie Joe's table. "No offense, dude," he shouted to Jake, "but you should probably go sit over there now."

As Jake got up, Hannah gave him a quick kiss on the cheek.

"You're a Phonie now," she said, "but I still like you."

Everyone laughed, then kept chanting.

Except me.

And nobody seemed to care.

A TRUE FRIEND

So the Cavemen decided to stick together and stick to the deal, but I didn't feel like celebrating. And at recess, I didn't really feel like hanging around with them, or with anyone for that matter.

Everyone was mad at me for how I acted toward Jake, but nobody was more mad than me. Because when I thought about it, even though my deal with Jane had been very clear—get *ten* friends to give up their phones for *one whole week*—she probably wouldn't have cared if one person dropped out toward the end. But now, I had to figure out what I was going to do: either tell Jane what had happened and risk her canceling the deal, or not tell her and feel incredibly guilty about lying.

Ugh.

I was sitting on a swing by myself, trying to figure out what to do, when I heard a voice behind me.

"Are you okay?"

I turned around to see Eliza standing there.

I couldn't believe it. Eliza! Two weeks ago, I'd thought she was just another unbelievably pretty but shallow girl. But she was a lot more than that. And right at that moment, she was a true friend.

I tried to smile. "I guess. I don't know. Not really."

"Well, that's a clear answer," Eliza said, sitting in the swing next to me. "You want to talk about it?"

As it turned out, I did. I told her everything: the concert, the accidental text to Nareem, the tension with Becca about writing songs, the deal with Jane, lying to her about cell phones ruining your brain, Nareem not wanting to talk to me for a while, me getting mad at Jake because now Jane would never sing my song—all of it.

It felt so good to talk about it, even though the whole thing made me sound kind of like a terrible person.

Eliza just sat there, listening. After I was finished, I waited for her to walk away, or get mad at me, or at least shake her head in disappointment.

Instead, she said one simple thing.

"How can I help?"

That was kind of amazing.

And I realized exactly what I had to do.

"Do you think maybe you could ask Nareem to get one last letter to Jane for me? I'm not sure he wants anything to do with me right now, but I need to write to Jane and tell her what happened."

She nodded. "Of course."

I hopped off the swing and stared up into the white sun. "Thanks, Eliza. For everything. You're a really great person, and I'm glad I finally know that."

"Write the letter today," she said, "and I will give it to Nareem after school."

She gave me a little hug and walked away. I think she sensed that I wanted to be alone.

She was right. I did want to be alone.

But not really.

THE LAST LETTER

Dear Jane,

I almost made it.

I tried, I really did. I had ten friends, and we had all given up our phones for almost a week. Then, this morning, one of the people took his phone back. But nobody even got that mad at him.

Except me.

Because instead of thinking about the group, I thought of myself, and how this might mess up the deal I had with you.

I acted badly.

It was worse because we've all become really good friends this week, even though some of us barely knew each other before. And everyone else was so nice to Jake. They understood that he tried his hardest. But I didn't. I blew it. Like I said, I was thinking that now you wouldn't play my song at your next concert. And the sad thing is, I'll bet you would have played it anyway.

Which reminds me, I have to tell you something else. You know how you asked me if I was working on the music to my song, and I said I was? Well, I was lying. I actually haven't written any music to it at all. I tried, but nothing happened. I wanted to play it at our talent show on Saturday night, but that's not going to happen. And so it turns out, I don't have a song for you to play at your next concert anyway.

So obviously, I know that all this means our deal is off.

Which I totally get.

But thank you SO MUCH for everything you did for me. I still feel so lucky that I met you. I'm sorry I let you down. I have a lot to work on and you are my inspiration.

Thanks again.

Your fan,

Katie Friedman

CREATING SOMETHING

That night, of course, the melody came to me in about five minutes.

> *How do you*
> *Speak the words*
> *That you never thought would be spoken?*

> *How do you*
> *Break the heart*
> *That never has been broken?*

I was in my room thinking about the whole day, starting with my locker being broken into, and thinking Charlie Joe did it, and finding out Jake stole his own phone back, and yelling at him, and Eliza being such a good friend, and the letter I'd written to Jane, and how I'd probably never hear from her again.

Then I picked up my guitar, and I started singing, and the music just came out.

How do you
Find the strength
To finally walk out the door?

How do you
Tell the one you loved
You don't love them anymore?

An hour later, I had the whole song. I don't know how it happened. It just did. I guess that's what creating something is. It's waiting for whatever it is to be ready to pour out of you, and then when it's time, getting out of the way and letting it happen.

I remembered when I wrote the words to the song. It was the night I sent my very last text, that horrible mistake that broke Nareem's heart. Now here I was, finally able to write the music, on another night I was really upset. Did that mean I could only create things when I was sad? I hoped not. I wanted to write songs, but I didn't want to have to live a miserable life to do it.

But that was something to worry about some other time. For now, I had written a song! And I was excited to teach it to the band at rehearsal the next night. Maybe Becca and the girls would love it, and we could even play it at the talent show!

For the first time all day, I felt something like hope.

TWO APOLOGIES

The next morning I went to find Jake and apologize. I looked all over the school, then found him and Hannah standing by my locker.

"Hi," I said.

"Hi," they said.

They waited. I had a whole speech prepared in my head, but I forgot every word.

"I'm really, really sorry for screaming at you," I stammered finally.

Jake said, "It's okay," and I felt a huge weight lift off my shoulders.

We stood there kind of awkwardly for a second, then I said, "Um, what are you guys doing here? By my locker, I mean?"

Jake held out his phone. "I wanted to give this back to you."

I stared down at it. "Are you sure?"

"I'm sure," Jake said.

I still didn't understand. "Really?"

"You were totally a jerk yesterday," Hannah said to me. "But you know what? Jake kind of deserved it in a way. If he wanted his phone back, he could have just asked for it. But he was scared and ashamed and so he didn't. He went into your locker without asking, which is definitely not cool."

"You're not the only one who's sorry," Jake told me. "I owe you an apology, too. And I want to stick to the deal. One for all and all for one, right?" He smiled.

I took the phone. "Okay!"

I'm ashamed to admit that the next thing I thought about was somehow getting word to Jane that our deal was back on.

But I'm proud to admit that that thought only lasted a second—maybe three—and then I banished it from my head.

Forever.

THE LAST REHEARSAL

At the end of the school day, I went to my locker, got the bag of phones, and brought them home. I was going to give them back to everybody at the talent show the next night. I went to my closet to put the bag inside, but first, I pulled out my phone and stared at it. Who knew such a little device could cause so much drama? My fingers itched as I thought about checking my texts, and taking a picture of the bag of phones and posting it online, congratulating the Cavemen on finishing the week. But I put the phone back in the bag. I could wait one more day.

That night, I got to Becca's house early for rehearsal, as usual. I wanted to talk to Becca privately and play her the song I wrote. But when I arrived, I was surprised to see Sammie and Jackie already there.

I hadn't seen much of Sammie over the last couple of days, since she was a Phonie.

"Hey," I said to her.

"What's up?" she said.

I said hi to the other girls, but I could tell that something was a little weird, like I was interrupting a private conversation or something.

"Everything okay?" I asked.

"Everything's great!" Becca said, oversmiling. "Let's get to work. We've got a lot to do."

"Yeah," Jackie said. "Big show tomorrow night! We've got to nail down our songs."

I got out my guitar. "I'm ready, you guys," I said, relieved to get to the music. "Let's do this."

We rehearsed for about an hour, going through about six songs, then we decided that the ones we'd play at the talent show would be "I Love Rock and Roll" by Joan Jett and "California Gurls" by Katy Perry.

"We're gonna rock it!" Sammie said from behind her drum set. Everyone laughed, including me. I actually felt happy and so relieved. The power of music is amazing. Which might be why I felt bold enough to say what I said next.

"Listen you guys, I wanted to let you know that I finished my song last night." They all stopped fiddling with their instruments and looked at me. "I'm not saying we should do it at the talent show or anything, but I just want to play it for you guys, so you can tell me if it's any good or not."

Jackie noodled on her keyboard. "I'm sure it's good. You don't need us to tell you that."

"I bet it's amazing," Becca said.

"You're really talented," Sammie added.

Suddenly I felt this overpowering need to play it for them. Just to share it with *someone*.

"I don't know how talented I am, you guys," I said. "I've never written a whole song before. It's short! I just want to play it for you!"

"Of course," Becca said. "Of course you can play it for us. But can you maybe play it for us later? Right now we should really rehearse the songs we're playing tomorrow night."

"Okay," I said. "No problem."

We played "California Gurls," and it sounded really good. Then we played "I Love Rock and Roll!" which also sounded really good.

"What should we do now?" I asked.

The rest of the band looked at each other.

"We should probably run the two songs again, just to nail them down," Sammie said.

"Why?" I said. "They sound great. We don't want to over-rehearse."

Jackie, Sammie, and Becca looked at each other, as if trying to figure out who should talk next.

"It's awesome you wrote a song," Sammie said, finally.

"But I think we should probably just use this rehearsal to work on our talent show stuff."

"Yeah," Jackie agreed.

Becca nodded, without looking at me.

"I need to go to the bathroom," I said.

"Okay," said Becca.

I went into the bathroom and locked the door. I took about twenty deep breaths. I made myself calm down. Then I headed back down to Becca's basement, promising myself I'd play those two songs a zillion times, if they wanted to.

But when I was on the steps, I heard them talking. More like whispering.

I stopped.

"I thought you were going to tell her," I heard Jackie say.

"I didn't have a chance," Becca answered.

"At this point, we'll just wait until after the talent show," Sammie said. "It will be fun and a good way to end."

"CHICKMATE's farewell tour," said Jackie, giggling.

"Do you think she'll be mad?" Sammie's voice.

"Maybe at first," Becca said. "But she'll get over it. She might even thank us. This isn't the group she wants, and we're not the musicians she wants."

"She wants to be Jane Plantero," agreed Sammie. "I just want to bang on a few drums between field hockey practices."

They all laughed.

"Jane Plantero! Good luck with that."

I wasn't sure who said that last thing, because I was already on my way back up the stairs and out the door.

THE LONG WALK HOME

Walking home from Becca's house, I went over the whole last week in my head. Was it only a week ago that I'd gone to the concert with Nareem? That was hard to believe.

It should have been the greatest week of my life.

But instead it turned into one of the worst.

How could it have gone so wrong?

I was trying to figure that out when I looked around and realized something.

It was getting late.

Then I realized something else.

I wasn't going to make it home before dark.

I started running, which considering my general state of fitness, is not necessarily a good idea. After about five minutes, I started breathing so hard I thought I was going to keel over.

Then I did something pretty hilarious.

I reached into my pocket to call my mom.

Oh, right. NO CELL PHONE.

Which is when I got a little scared.

It's not like I'm a baby: I actually even like horror movies. But I'd never been far from home at nighttime with no way to get in touch with anyone before. It wasn't a good feeling.

I remembered what Charlie Joe said earlier in the week, when he held up his phone and said there was a call for me.

What if something bad actually happened?

I tried to put that out of my head.

I was on a busy road, with a very thin sidewalk. Cars whizzed by me, the fumes from their exhaust pipes blasting stinky heat up my nose.

Oh, and did I mention it started to rain?

I walked for a few minutes, then jogged for a few minutes, and realized I still had about two miles to go. And there wasn't even a gas station or anything between here and there.

I was trying to decide if maybe I should just go up to a random house and ask to use the phone when a car pulled up beside me. The window went down, and I heard a male voice.

"Do you need a ride?"

I didn't turn and look, because people say never make eye contact with a stranger. I just shook my head. "No, thank you."

"It's getting dark out here, young lady," the voice said. "Are you sure?"

"Yes, I'm sure." For a minute I was tempted to ask this person for their cellphone, but I resisted.

"Okay," the man said, and off he went.

I started to cry a little bit, and started getting mad at myself. How could I ever have thought giving up my cell phone was a good idea? What was wrong with me?!

Another car pulled up. I started to run. The car was right behind me. I tried to run faster, but I couldn't. I was wet, and tired, and defeated. I stopped and turned. I would accept their ride, whoever it was. I would just have to hope that the person driving wasn't an escaped criminal.

The car window rolled down.

"Katie? Oh my God, there you are! We've been looking all over for you!"

It was Becca and her father.

I started to cry for real.

I'd never been so happy to see someone in my whole life.

With the possible exception of Jane Plantero.

PRETTY TYPICAL MIDDLE SCHOOL STUFF

I was drier and calmer by the time Becca's dad dropped me home.

My mom gave me a huge hug. "Oh my goodness. What were you thinking?!?!"

Before I could answer, Becca did.

"It wasn't her fault," she told my mom. "Katie overheard me and the other girls saying mean things about her behind her back."

"You weren't saying mean things," I said. "You were just trying to figure out how to tell me you didn't want to be in the band anymore. I overreacted."

We both tried to smile. "It's been a long week," I added.

"Well, listen," my mom said. "This all sounds like pretty typical middle school stuff to me. And regardless of what happens with the band, you guys have a big gig tomorrow night, and you need to get some rest."

"Nice use of the word *gig*, Mom," I said.

"I try," she said.

I walked Becca to the door. We looked at each other.

"Are we still playing tomorrow night?" I asked her.

She looked unsure. "Do you want to?"

There were so many ways to answer that question. One of which was, "Not in a million years." Another of which was, "I wouldn't miss it for the world."

The truth lay somewhere in the middle.

"I think so," I said. "I think we should."

"People would think it was weird if we didn't show up," Becca agreed.

"And Ms. Ferrell would be mad," I added, and we both tried to laugh.

We stood there for another minute. There seemed to be so much to say, but we decided not to say any of it. Sometimes, part of communicating is keeping quiet.

So all we ended up saying was, "See you tomorrow."

PRESHOW

The next day went by so slowly, it felt like it took three weeks.

Finally, at six o'clock, it was time to go. I got my guitar and amp and headed out to the car. My mom was halfway down our road when I yelled, "Stop!" and told her to go back.

She drove back to the house, and I ran inside to get the bag of phones.

♥ ♥ ♥

When I got to the school, I was nervous to go inside. Part of me was wondering if Jackie and Sammie would actually show up. But there they were, hanging out in the orchestra room with Becca, warming up with everyone else.

When they saw me coming, they looked a little nervous, too.

"Are you okay?" Sammie said.

"We were worried about you," Jackie said.

"I'm fine," I told them. "I'm great."

Awkward minute-long silence.

"We didn't know how to tell you," Jackie said. "Becca said you would be so upset, and none of us wanted to make you upset."

Sammie nodded. "It's just that we're not as good musicians as you are."

I shook my head. "I don't blame you guys," I said. "Becca called me 'bossy' the other day, and she was right. I wanted to turn CHICKMATE into *my* band, instead of *our* band. I shouldn't have done that, and I'm sorry."

"I'm sorry, too," Jackie whispered.

Becca touched my shoulder. "We're really proud of you for writing a song."

"When you become a famous musician some day," Jackie said, "I want front-row seats."

"Wow, I'm glad that's over with," I said. "Now we can get back to the business of being incredibly nervous about the show."

We laughed, and felt better, and started to relax.

Meanwhile, Sammie was nodding her head. "Okay, now I get it."

We looked at her. "Get what?" I said.

"Now I get what life is like without a cell phone."

The rest of us looked at each other, confused.

"This conversation!" Sammie went on. "If you guys had your phones, we would have had this conversation last night on text, and it would have been so different. This is so much cooler! This is real connection!" She took out her phone and handed it to me. "I want to give up my phone, too!"

I laughed. "Well, you're a little too late," I said. Then I held out the bag of phones to Becca and Jackie. "Congratulations. You made it."

They hesitated, then peered wide-eyed into the bag, almost as though they were looking at buried treasure.

"Wow," Becca said. "There they are."

"I don't think I've ever seen a more beautiful sight," Jackie said.

Then they laughed, grabbed their phones, and stared at them like they were long-lost friends.

"This may be the greatest day of my life," Becca said.

Frowning, Sammie watched them excitedly turn on their phones. "I don't get it, you guys," she said. "Didn't you love not having your phones? Weren't you incredibly proud of being Cavemen?"

"I did love being a Caveman," Becca said, turning on her phone. "But I love being a Phonie more."

Then she quickly took a picture of Sammie's shocked face.

HAPPY REUNIONS

I spent the rest of the preshow finding the other Cavemen and giving them all their phones back. Everyone pretty much had the same reaction as Becca and Jackie: pure joy. Probably the best reaction was Eliza's, who squealed, jumped for joy, turned on her phone, took a selfie, and posted it online, all in about three seconds.

"I've missed you so much!" she cooed to her phone, petting it like a puppy.

The last people I returned phones to were Jake and Hannah. I found them sitting in the auditorium, talking to each other and holding hands, waiting for the show to start.

I watched them let go of each

Selfie

other's hands, take their phones and turn them on—Jake had a bunch of texts come in, probably all from his mom. Then I watched them each stare at their phones for a few minutes. Finally I sat down next to them.

"Can I ask you guys something?"

They looked up from their phones and waited.

"Three minutes ago, you were talking and holding hands. Then the minute I gave you your phones back, you started ignoring each other and kind of went into your own worlds." I stopped for a second, trying to figure out how to put it. "Isn't that the whole reason we gave up our phones in the first place?"

Hannah put her phone in her backpack.

"We gave up our phones for a week because it seemed like an interesting thing to try, and we wanted to see if we could do it," she said. "And we did. But I would never give it up, like, forever." She looked at Jake. "And you don't have to worry about us. We communicate just fine."

Jake was answering a text, though, and didn't even hear her.

SHOWTIME

We were scheduled to perform right after Louie Capistrano, who recited the National Anthem backward.

Brave the of home the and

Free the of land the O'er

It was pretty amazing. He knew the whole thing by heart. By the time he got to *See You Can Say O*, the place was going nuts.

"How are we going to top that?" Becca whispered to me, backstage.

"Good question," I answered.

Mr. Radonski, our very intense gym teacher, was the host of the show. "How about another hand for Louie and his 'Star-Spangled Backward'!" he yelled, and the place went crazy again. Oh, great.

He made the calm-down motion with his hands. "And

now, let's welcome to the stage, the rock and roll sounds of CHICKMATE!"

Everyone clapped as we ran onto the stage and grabbed our instruments. I adjusted the mike. "Hey, everyone, what's up? We're CHICKMATE," I said, trying to be as cool as Jane Plantero but obviously not even coming close. "We're going to start with some Joan Jett." I nodded to Sammie behind the drums, and she counted off: "1 -2-3- 4!"

As we launched into the song, people started cheering. Becca and I sang in unison. The people in the audience who knew the song sang along with every word. We sounded really good, I think. Everyone in the band smiled at one another as we played. It felt great.

Music is so powerful. Whether you're listening to it or playing it yourself, it is amazing how it can take you to a better place. I think that's why I really want to be a musician, to write the songs that help other people get to that place.

We finished "I Love Rock and Roll" and went right into "California Gurls." By the time we finished that one, the crowd was just as loud as when Louie Capistrano did his crazy backward trick.

Sammie came out from behind her drums to the front of the stage, and we all did a group hug.

"We did it!" Jackie yelled.

"That was amazing!" Sammie yelled.

"I can't believe it!" Becca yelled.

Then they all waited for me to say something.

"You guys are awesome," I said finally.

We hugged again, then went down to the front of the stage. We held hands and took a bow. The crowd cheered even louder.

I soaked it all in, even though a voice inside my head kept repeating one thing:

CHICKMATE is over.

ENCORE

While the audience was still clapping, Mr. Radonski came out with a microphone in his hand. I waved one last time and started to leave the stage, but Becca stopped me.

"Wait just a second," she said. Then she nodded to Mr. Radonski.

"As a special treat," he said into the mike, "we would like Katie Friedman to play her new original song that she's just written."

I heard him speaking, but I wasn't sure I understood the words. My heart started to race, and electric currents started jolting my skin. I turned to Becca.

"What did he just say?"

She was smiling. "I told you I wanted to hear the song, didn't I? Well, let's hear it."

The crowd started cheering again. Some kids were chanting "Katie! Katie! Katie!" I stood there, in shock.

After a minute, I was finally able to pull myself together and pick up my guitar. The crowd got quiet, and I stepped up to the mike.

"Wow," I said. Then, "Um." After a few more seconds, "Okay."

Pretty rock star of me, huh?

But gradually, my heartbeat started to return to a human level, and my nervous system was no longer on fire, and I started to calm down.

Okay. You can do this.

"I've never played this song for anyone before," I said, and the crowd roared. "I just finished writing it actually."

For some reason my eyes searched out Nareem in the audience. I found him, staring back at me with a weird half-smile on his face. I didn't have time to try and figure out what it meant, though.

"I hope you like it."

I strummed a few chords on my guitar to make sure it was in tune, then played the first chord of the song.

I closed my eyes and sang.

How do you
Speak the words
That you never thought would be spoken?

213

How do you
Break the heart
That never has been broken?

How do you
Find the strength
To finally walk out the door?

How do you
Tell the one you loved
You don't love them anymore?

I want to know.
I need to know.
I have to know right now.
I'm on my knees
So someone please
Please come show me how.

My eyes were still closed. I think I was afraid to look out into the audience. But I could hear just fine. And when the crowd let out a deafening roar, my eyes jolted open. What was going on?

A voice behind me started singing.

How do you
Look someone in the eye
When you're not sure what you want to see

I knew the voice. It kept singing.

How do you
Say the words
There is no more you and me.

I turned around and saw her.
Jane Plantero.
She was right there, on the stage of my middle school auditorium, walking toward me. She was wearing a white T-shirt and torn jeans. In one hand she held a microphone, and in the other, she was holding the crumpled-up lyric sheet that I'd sent her a week before. She was smiling. And she was singing.

How do you
Resist the urge
To hide behind a screen?

How do you
Know it's time
To give up the machine?

Even though she didn't exactly know the melody, she still sounded AMAZING. I guess that's why she's a rock star.

I stared, disbelieving, as Jane reached me. She put her arm around me. "Join me for this last chorus," she said.

So I did.

I want to know.
I need to know.
I have to know right now.
I'm on my knees
So someone please
Please come show me how.

Then Jane gestured to the wings of the stage and the rest of the band came out. We sang the last part of the song again.

How do you
Resist the urge
To hide behind a screen?

How do you
Know it's time
To give up the machine?

I want to know.
I need to know.
I have to know right now.

I'm on my knees
So someone please
Please come show me how.

This time I kept my eyes wide open.

JANE'S PLEA

After the song ended, the crowd kept cheering and hollering for about six minutes straight. I just kept staring at Jane, still not able to believe she was standing next to me, having just *sung my song.*

Finally, she hushed the crowd.

"I need to tell you guys something," she said into the microphone. "First of all, it's great to be back here at East-port Middle. This auditorium is where I got my start as a singer."

The crowd went crazy.

(From now on, I'm not going to tell you every time the crowd went crazy. Just assume they did, pretty much after every sentence.)

"But that's not why I'm here. I'm here because I made a deal with this girl right here. Katie." As she put her arm around me, I noticed that three-quarters of the audience already had their cell phones out, recording everything. I wondered if Jane would say anything about that.

"I'm not a big fan of cell phones, and texting, and all that stuff," she went on. "I know technology is amazing. I know it's real useful and stuff. But it's no good if it helps you hide from one another. It's no good if it isolates you from one another. It's no good if it makes you mean and insensitive to one another." She smiled at all the people holding up their cell phones. "And it's no good if it turns you from a doer to a watcher."

She turned to me. "So when I met this girl, and she told me she wanted to write and sing songs, I told her, if she and ten friends gave up their cell phones for a week, I would play her song at my next concert." She raised her arms to the crowd. "It just turned out that *this* was my next concert!"

At that point, the crowd did their best imitation of an insane asylum.

"Here's the last thing I'll say," Jane said, talking into the mike but looking at me. "You've got two good friends in Eliza and Nareem. They sent me that letter you wrote, saying you didn't live up to your end of the bargain. But they also wrote me a note of their own, telling me about how upset you were, and what a good person you are, and asking if maybe I wouldn't mind coming here and singing with you." Jane turned around and looked at the rest of the band. "And when these guys told me backstage that you'd actually finished *your* song, I knew that we were in business."

I stared at Becca. "You met Jane backstage??? You *knew*?!"

She grinned. "When you were running around giving everybody their phones back," she said.

"So finally," Jane said. "If everyone whose name I call can come up onstage. From what I understand, you call yourselves Cavemen. Sounds like a good name for a band."

Jane called out all our names. Eliza. Ricky. Tiffany. Amber. Hannah. Jake. Phil. Celia. Becca. Jackie. Katie.

And when all the Cavemen were up onstage, we took a bow.

"I had a great time," Jane said, waving goodbye to the crowd. "See you on tour!"

As we headed off stage to one last deafening round of applause, Jane pulled me aside.

"Becca told me about last night," she said. "How you heard them talking about not really wanting to be in the band anymore."

"Yeah," I said, embarrassed. "I guess I'm a little too intense for them."

"You're passionate!" Jane said. "That's a good thing, never forget that."

"I guess so. It just felt like they were talking about me behind my back, though, so I just left."

Jane smiled. "That's a drag for sure, but that kinda stuff helps us remember that secrets and lies and talking behind people's backs are bad news, no matter whether they come from somebody's phone, or somebody's mouth."

I thought about that for a second. She was absolutely right.

Jane put her guitar back in her case. "One last thing," she said, heading for the door. "A lot of people write songs only when they're upset. But that's not a great way to be. If you want to be a songwriter, you gotta write 'em when you're sad, happy, and everything in between."

She took a long swig of water and gave me a hug that I will remember forever.

"Because music is great," she said, "but happiness is better."

EPILOGUE

KATIE FRIEDMAN'S FIRST TEXT

Don't control—connect.
Don't attack—accept.
Gifts are for the giving.
Life is for the living.

"It's great to be here!" Jane yelled. "PLAIN JANE is in the house!

It was two months later, and Plain Jane was back on tour.

We were there, of course. Cavemen, Phonies, members of CHICKMATE, you name it, we were all there. Before the show, Kit had given a bunch of us a backstage tour—even though it was supposed to be just for Cavemen, somehow Charlie Joe snuck his way in and walked out with an entire bowl of M&M'S. I yelled at him, of course, but gladly stuffed my face with them all through the concert.

I looked around at everyone. Phil and Celia were arm in arm, swaying back and forth to the music. Hannah and Jake were laughing and holding hands. Becca, Jackie, and Sammie were singing along at the top of their lungs. And Ricky, Nareem, Eliza, Timmy, Pete, Tiffany, and Amber were all in a big circle, slow-dancing together.

Wow. Music really does do amazing things to people.

Almost the entire audience was videoing the concert with their phones, by the way, but Jane didn't seem to mind so much this time. Maybe she figured she didn't want to be a nag, or maybe she just thought talking about it again would have been boring, or maybe Nareem's dad had convinced her that people posting videos of her concerts on YouTube was good for business. Whatever the reason, Jane was just up there having fun, singing the incredible songs that she wrote when she was sad, happy, and everything in between.

The concert was unbelievable. Being there with my friends was unbelievable. The brand-new Plain Jane tour jacket that Kit had given me was unbelievable. And knowing that I could actually consider Jane Plantero a friend was maybe the most unbelievable thing of all.

Charlie Joe, meanwhile, was taking pictures every five seconds and texting them to me.

"Cut it out," I said.

"You'll thank me later," he answered.

"We'll see."

"Well, can't you just text me back so I know you got them?"

"Very funny," I said.

Charlie Joe shrugged. "Well, you can't blame a guy for trying."

Then he shook his head and laughed.

Because here's the thing: Ever since no-phone-week ended, I had my phone back with me—like most human beings—but I still hadn't sent a single text to anybody. Not one, since the last horrible text I sent to Nareem by accident. Not to Charlie Joe, not to Eliza, not even to my parents. I just couldn't bring myself to do it. In the meantime, everyone had given up trying to text me, or trying to get me to text them. Everyone except for Charlie Joe, that is.

Two hours into the concert though, just before the last encore, my phone buzzed again. I looked down, shaking my head, thinking it was another picture from Charlie Joe. But it wasn't.

It was a text from Nareem.

I stared down at it.

HAVING FUN?

I looked at him. He looked back.

We smiled.

I held my phone in my hands for what seemed like a lifetime before I finally decided to text him back.

YES.

Charlie Joe's Top Ten Reasons Why Texting is Awesome

By Charlie Joe Jackson

1. It's a way to read and write, without having to actually read and write.
2. It helps parents and kids communicate with each other. Like, twenty times a day.
3. Phone call + Noisy game or concert = Doesn't work.
4. You can tell people you speak another language. BRB TTYL LOL!
5. Moms can't overhear texts.
6. Ten people can have a conversation without getting annoyed that they're interrupting each other.
7. You can win a contest just by pushing a few buttons!
8. It's quieter than yelling.
9. I just love that sound my phone makes when a text comes in. It's a sound that says, "Somebody cares."
10. It's great exercise for your thumbs.

All Charlie Joe.
All the time.

READ THE SERIES THAT STARTED IT ALL . . .

Charlie Joe Jackson's
Guide to Not Reading
978-1-250-00337-9

Charlie Joe Jackson's
Guide to Extra Credit
978-1-250-01670-6

Check out all of my titles on cjjbookshelf.com!

Charlie Joe Jackson's
Guide to Summer Vacation

978-1-62672-031-2

Charlie Joe Jackson's
Guide to Making Money

978-1-59643-840-8

COMING SOON!
Charlie Joe Jackson's
Guide to Planet Girl

978-1-59643-841-5

Also available from Tommy Greenwald:

Sometime you just want to be a kid!

978-1-250-05687-0